T0354695

The Hornets Nest

The Hornets Nest

Johnques Lupoe

THE HORNETS NEST

iUniverse books may be ordered through booksellers or by contacting:

iUniverse
1663 Liberty Drive
Bloomington, IN 47403
www.iuniverse.com
844-349-9409

ISBN: 978-1-6632-3352-3 (sc)
ISBN: 978-1-6632-3353-0 (e)

Library of Congress Control Number: 2021925188

Print information available on the last page.

iUniverse rev. date: 12/09/2021

Prologue

It all started the summer of 75. Young Eve Mae watched her mother and brother die. With her brother only being a few years older than she was, she took it hard. Her mother was never really home. And when she was it was with a different guy. Not really knowing what she slept with so many men until they both died.

With Henry being her only sibling, he taught her the ways of a hustler. Watching him beef with crazy Deane form the block, over their mother put everything in place. Deane was a well-known pimp on the Metropolitan track. Their mother was getting pimped by Deane. And Henry was tired of seeing her come home with black eyes and bruise.

Now that the only two people she cared about was dead, she had no one to turn to. Running back to their two bed room apartment and locked the door. She took her book bag and flipped it upside down. Dumping everything out of it before shooting off to their room. Snatching the covers off the Queen size bed that they shared. And begun pulling out all of Henry's money that he use to stash there.

Then Rushed to one of his old shoe boxes, where he kept his drugs. Opening it up to find two oz's of weed and one oz of crack Rock. Taking the book bag with everything in and hide it inside of the oven. Sliding down the oven door until she was sitting on the floor. Crying her heart out until she fell asleep.

90's

Having Rob Bass "It takes two" blaring through the speakers as she danced around on the floor. Celebrating her new connect with some Asians. Getting pure cocaine for an unbelievable prize. Knowing that she was about to be even richer than ever. As the night got young and the party started to die down, she pasted out samples in green nick bags.

With the Asians on her side with the cocaine and having heroin at her deplorer if needed. She knew it was no way for her to lose. Locking up her house, then entering a bedroom. Seeing her two kids knock out cold, brought and even bigger smile on her face. Kissing them both on the forehead, while covering them up.

2000

"Sticky, Honey get yall ass in here."

"What's up ma?" Santana asked.

Yes mother, hope answered.

"I got someone I want yall to meet."

"Man ma it better not be another buster" Santana blurted out.

"Girl watch your mouth."

"Who is it Moma?" Hope asked.

"This is Eddie, Eddie these are my girls, Hope and Santana or you can them Honey and sticky."

"Hey aint you the guy that work at that restaurant" Hope asked

"And you must be Honey" Eddie replied

As she introduce them into her mastery man that she has been dating for four years now. Santana checked him out, looking him up and down from head to toe. Eve mae was coming to an end of being a Queen pin and wanted a steady man around the house for.

For the girls. Thinking that now was the best time to bring him around. He was a hustler just like she was and they got alone so well. Hell they even did business together and with each other.

Over time and years passing by Queen cut by on her shipment and Eddie felt some type of way. Not wanting her to quit the dope game, because of the connect he was getting with the heroin through her. Queen realized that it was love anymore it was just about the money. Cutting him off and moving on with her life plans.

She knew what was best for her and daughters. Teaching Honey how to use what she got to get what she needed. And Teaching sticky the hustle on everything. Knowing that they both took after her in different ways, she had to tech them what they was good at.

Chapter 1

Queen B: T. H. N

"Knock, knock, knock" "Go ahead and place you bets while I get the door". while walking to the door Eva mae, checked on the chicken and fries she had just dropped in the grease, "Who is it?

"It's 5 duce" Unlocking and opening the door 5 duce stood there counting money

"What can I help you with tonight?" "I'm trying to break the bank tonight and I want one of your famous burgers" "Ok well come on in"

5 duce walked around to the gambling area and took a seat at the black jack table. The bootleg / gambling house were jumping like Aways. Evamae aka Queen B was known for her mean hustle game. You would think she was a younsta by the way she look and move. Queen B stood at 5'3 and weigh 125, nice fat ass, small but perkie breast, green eyes and sandy brown hair to match her peacan tan skin tone. If you didn't know any better you would think that she was 30 and not 53.

And she had two daughters Honey and Sticky, you would think they all was sisters. As Queen B made her way back around to check on her gambling tables and to drop off their orders she got a call.

"Hold one second please" Queen B stated as she placed the phone back in her pocket.

"Ok I'm back and who's calling"

"Umm this is Tuck"

"Ok how can I help you"

"Well I was told that you was the go to lady whatever and I got a nigga in my way but I can't"

Stopping Tuck before he could finish his statement Queen B told him to meet her tomorrow at 7:00 at the OLG restaurant. Hanging up the phone after telling him what to do when he got to the Restaurant. Queen went back to handling the gambl8ing house. Money was rolling in good as usual. And like any other gambling house you always have one drunk that want to show out.

Tim had done got drink as always and done lost all of his money. Now he is crying about going home to his baby moma without the rent money. Tim begin laying all over the tables trying to pick fights with people. Evamae grabbed Tim by his arm and pulled him towards the door. Jerking a way from her then taking a swing at her. evamae step back and looked at him not believing that fool just did that.

"Ok Tim that's your first and last time swing at me now gone leave"

"Bitch I aint going nowhere until I get my money back"

"Well nigga if you don't have no money to bet with they you know the rules."

"Fuck them rules I want my shit back bitch"

"Oh I got yo bitch, you not about to keep disrespecting me in my shit"

Queen B ran to her little safe spot and grabb her 357 magnum. Racing back through the living room, everybody panicky got out the way. 5 duce jumped up and ran behind her, Eva mae pulled back up on Tim and aimed the 357 at his head.

"Bitch I'm gone show you why they call me Queen B"

"Wait! Wait! Wait! Don't do it shawty I'll handle it" 5duce shouted out Jumping in between her and Tim, 5duce told Tim to get out the hose before shit got out of hand. Tim laughed then asked 5duce if he wanted some smoke. "This aint what you want CUZ"

"Well come on out here and show me, cause somebody go to pay me."

5 duce open the door and waited for Tim to walk out then shut it behind him. Hitting him with the oldest trick in the book. Turning around to walk back to the gambling table, Evamae stopped him and told him that he didn't have to do that.

"I'm not about to let a pretty lil thing like you get hurt"

"Boy I'm old enough to be your moma so don't try it"

"What you mean Shawty you aint nothing but 30 something"

"Thanks but I been out of 30's but I'm gone give you a free meal just for stepping up"

"Hel let me get another round of liquor to go with that plate if you don't mind while 5 duce walked back to the table. Queen fixed him up a nice little shot and a plate. Everything what back to normal? More people came in and out, some just to buy plates or liquor. And others to gamble, everybody knew they had to be in the house before her cut off point. But Queen kept everything on a schedule, so she wouldn't draw heat to herself.

T. H. N: Honey

"Yo! yo! yo! give it up for H2 aka Hard Hitter G, that was his smashing new hit "B. B. A" Dj extreme shouted out over the microphone as H2 walked off the stage. As Dj extreme spinned the next song Honey made her way through the crowed. With money on her mind she plays it cool sliding up next to H2.

"Umm excuse me, H2 right"

"Yeah that's me and who you G with you fine ass?"

"I'm Honey and I just wanted to let you know that I was feeling that song

"Well, good that's what made it for, for bad bitches like you"

"So have you made it big time yet"

Somewhat but fuck all that, let's get out of here and go somewhere nice"

"That sounds good to me"

As they made their way over to the V. I. P, H2 hitting Honey with all kind of lingo. But he just didn't know who he was dealing with. Honey was a master of persuasion and a hell of a con artist. Before they could even get seated, Honey told H2 that she need to use the restroom. She took off inside the V. I. P area checking out all of the ballers. Walking inside the bathroom Honey walked over to the sink and mirror.

Adjusting her shirt so her breast could sit up and show a little bit more. Then made sure her hair was still straight and her breath was on point. Honey left out the rest room headed back to her new hustle. But before she could even make it back, her attention was caught by another baller. Passing by him with a subduing strut, the guy jumped off the cough and sprinted over to her before she got to far. Gently grasping her by her hand and giving it a little pull to make her stop.

Honey turned around with an light rude "Excuse you"

"Damn baby no need for the attitude, just want a minute of your time"

"Ok just a minute because I have someone waiting for me"

"Well they can wait a little bit longer come have a seat with me"

"I can't do that, I just told you had I some on waiting for me"

"Girl look whoever it is tell them come party too, well get money over here"

"I don't even know yo name"

"Shiid they call me Sosa"

"Sosa?!"

"Yeah that's me, so what's up, what you gone do?"

Before she could reply, she saw H2 watching her. Standing there shaking his head as if he knew she wasn't no good. H2 just turned his back on her and walked off. Sosa peeped the whole play and asked her was that who she was with.

"Yeah it was but you messed that up"

"Oh well fuck'em you with me for the night"

"Just like that?!"

"Yeah that way"

Laughing on the inside, Honey made him feel like he had done did something. as she took her seat, Sosa called for the waitress to come over. While waiting for her to pull up Sosa begun asking Honey a few question, just to get to know her. Every question he asked, Honey responded back with a quick lie like she'd been rehearsing them. The waitress walked up to Sosa and Honey, you guys ready to order.

"Umm can I get some peach Ciroc"

"Sure and for you sir"

"Yeah let me get a bottle of Ace the black bottle"

"Ok anything else?"

"That's it for now"

The waitress walked off and Sosa slide closer to Honey Rubbing on her thing and whispered in her ear, Sosa knew he had her in the bag.

Sticky: T. H. N

Walking through the club looking for Honey, guys were stopping Sticky left and right. Standing at 5'7 with a fat ass and mid-size tills, Dirty red skin tone, hazel brown eyes, jet Black hair with gray high lites. The Gucci dress she had on hugged her body and showed off all her curves. And her open toe red bottom, showed off her toe nail polish that matched her dress.

As she got closer to the V. I. P. she saw Honey all over some dude. "Such a hoe" Sticky thought to herself as she made her way back through the crowd. Feeling someone grab her ass, she quickly stop and turned around. To be standing face to face with a dark chocolate female. "Excuse me but did grab my ass"

"I'm sorry I couldn't help myself"

"Bitch you lucky you are cute, because you where about to get that ass beat"

"Umm I like that, you are fine and sassy"

"What's you name child?"

"Rashida but you can call me Shida"

"I'm Sticky"

"Damn that's a hell of a name to give someone. But I would like ot see how Sticky you can get" Rashida giggled.

Sticky grabbed Rashid by he hand and took her through crowd. Positioning herself so she could keep and eye on Honey and entertain Rashida at the same time.

Honey: T. H. N

"Oh my God" Honey busted out

"What's that?!" Sosa asked

"Nothing I just see my lil stocker in the club tonight"

"Oh yea do you want me to handle it, I'll send my team at him."

"No it's a female, she be trying to talk to me"

"Shiid tell her to come over"

"That's not a good idea"

"Ok if you say so"

Sosa what back to listening to the music while Honey sat in his lap. Waving at the little sister to let her know that she spotted her. Sticky throw her thumbs up back at her. Feeling good Sosa pulls Honey closer to him them, ask her if she wanted to get out of there. The liquor had Sosa ready to fuck something. Honey stood up and stuck her hand out signifying that she was down with leaving.

As they was leaving out of the V. I. P, Honey seen H2 headed their way. Not knowing what was on his mind she grabbed Sosa arm a little tighter. Making him look down at her, Honey just smiled. Sosa looked puzzled but when he raised his head back up he noticed H2 standing there.

"Lil bubby you bad and all but you ain't talking about shit" H2 shouted out

"Get yo weight up my nigga and you'll be able to keep you hoes" Sosa shoot back

"Oh nigga this Big Boss shit over here, fuck you mean"

"Yeah and it's Big B's we're here so you aint saying shit"

Walking off trying not to blow his high and the buzz from the liquor, Sosa just brushed him off. Headed got the club Honey looked over her shoulder to make sure they weren't being followed. Stepping outside Sosa had them pull his car out of V.I.P parking. Honey eyes got a buck when she seen the car, she knew he was a heavy hitta. As the valet opened up the Bentley coop doors, Honey slid right in.

"Aye Brittany you did say it didn't matter where we went right?" Sosa asked

"Yeah I'm with you tonight daddy" Honey replied.

"Ok cool"

Sosa reached in the back seat and picked up a small red bag. Sitting the bag in his lap and opened it up. Honey saw rolls Of money and something packaged in clear wrap. Honey act like she didn't see anything. Whole Sosa pulled out an all-black 40 cal. Sitting the 40 cal on the side of his console, while he put the bag back on the floor board. Looking at Honey then winked his eye as he drove off.

Sticky: T.H.N

"Sticky where we are going the club ain't about to close" Rashida asked

"Girl just comes with me"

Walking outside of the club just in time to see the candy Red Bentley drive off. "Come on my car is right over there." Sticky told Rashida as she took off walking fast. As they got inside of the 2018 Honda accord, Rashida was shocked. She thought she had struck, for a new girlfriend with a little money. Taking off to catch up to the Bentley, Sticky spots them a few cars up.

"Umm where are we going?"

"Don't know yeah so just sit back and ride."

"Damn you rude, but its making me wet"

Rashida reaches over and start rubbing on Sticky's leg. Trying to ease her way up her dress. Sticky looked over and told her don't ever try it. Rashida moved her hand and sat back in the seat. As they went in and out of traffic trying to keep up with the Bentley. Twenty minutes later they were pulling up at the court yard o Virginia Avenue. Parking two cars down from the Bentley, Sticky looked over at Rashida and told her to go get a room.

"Come in with me please"

"Al right"

Walking inside the hotel, she heard Honey and Sosa right behind them. Stepping to the side to let them go first.

She paid close attention to what room they were in. she was thinking that he would have got the pent house, with all of the money he was flashing. Sticky took Rashida up to their room. Which was the same room, but just a floor beneath Honey.

"Aye look go freshen up and I'll be right back"

"Where you going?"

"I'm going to the car to get my toys."

"Oooh ok, I like the way you Roll" Rashida said as she headed to the bathroom.

Sticky smacked her on the ass before she walked out the room. Racing down stairs and out the door to the car. She popped the truck and pulled out her tennis shoes and some black sweatpants putting the sweat pants on under the dress and sliding her feet into her black Air force ones. Grabbing her clock 9 and a few zippy ties, sticky close the trunk and head back up stairs. Making her way down the hall she confiscating a service cart.

Rolling it to the side of the door, Sticky knocks on it and cries out room service.

"I didn't order no room service" Sosa yelled from behind the door.

"No, I'm just here to drop off some fresh towels sir."

"Oh ok give me a min"

Sosa cracked the door and peeped out. Seeing the cart with towels and sheets on it, he told her to hold tight so he could take the chain off the door. As soon as she heard the chain come off and the door start to open, sticky got a running start and kicked the door. Hitting Sosa in the face with the door dazing him. Sticky Ran in and pulled out her 9mm. Aimed it at honey and told her to get over here.

"Please don't shoot me I don't even know him" Honey cried.

"Bitch I don't care if you know him or not, get over and tie him up."

As she made her way over, Sosa was coming around. He rushed Sticky and pinned her against the wall. Sticky shot him a quick knee to the nuts making him let her go. As he released her arms she came across his face with the pistol. Bring him to his knees, Sticky order for Honey to tie him up. As Honey zip tied Sosa hands behind his back, Sticky made Honey get on the floor right next to him. putting zip ties on Honey then tied up Sosa's feet.

Tearing up the room not finding a thing, Sticky stood there and looked around trying to see what she missed. Then it hit her, his pants were laying on the floor. Picking them up and going through them, she pulls out two stacks of folded money and his Bentley keys. Sticky smiled as she put the money and keys in her pocket.

"Tonight is my lucky night huh? Well I'm gone take this lil fine piece of ass you got here just in case try something stupid." Sticky said as she picked Honey up off the floor.

"Bitch I'm gonna kill you when I get free" Sosa yelled out as he rolled around trying to get free.

Kicking Sosa in the ribs as she walked out the room. Taking the stairs and out the side door, Sticky gave Honey her car keys and told her to follow her. As she pulled out of the hotel parking lot, she started rambling through the car. Finding the glock 40 and the red bag, she wanted to know what else was in the car. She drove down about 3 miles and pulled over into an empty parking lot. Hopping out and fully checking the car, she didn't find anything else. Making a quick call then grabbing everything out of the car and locked it up, then set the keys on the front tire. Jumping in the car with Honey, then hauled ass.

Chapter 2

Queen B: T.H.N

The next morning while doing inventory, Queen heard noises coming from up under the kitchen window. She took off and grabs her 357 and peeked out her door then went outside. Walking to the side of the house, she had seen Tim getting off the ground. Aiming the render at him, Queen asked him what was he doing outside of her house at this time of the morning.

"I never went home, I was to drunk to drive or walk" Tim replied

"Ok well make it on to your car, don't need no brain on my yard this early"

"I'm leaving no need to get all hostile"

Watching him stagger off her property and to his car, Queen walked back in the house. Once she made it back in the house she realized that Honey or Sticky wasn't at home. Picking up her cellphone off the counter and called Honey. With one hard on the phone up to her ear and the other on her hip still holding on to the 357. She was getting pissed because she know the girls knew better, Monday was the only day that they spend the morning together to plan out the week.

"Hello"

"Where yall little bitches at?"

"Ma we are on the way, Sticky is following behind me. We had to go get my car"

"What?! You know what I'm even going to ask."

"Well did you at least cook us breakfast?"

"Y'all just get to the house"

Hanging up the phone she heads a knock at the door. who he hell at my door a 9:30 in the morning "Queen mumbled to herself as she walked back to the front door. As she opened the door she startled the young guy standing at the door. "Can I help you"

"Umm I'm sorry Queen, I know its early but I need a box of blunts"

"I'm out of blunts but I got some wraps"

"Ok cool"

Walking away from the door in her pajamas, the young guy watched her ass jiggle while she walked. Licking his lips and gripping on himself, before he knew it he had done shouted out a damn!". Queen looked back with a puzzled look on her face. Seeing him standing there groping himself, she already knew what was wrong. Queen grabbed the wraps and took them back to him. As she gave the wraps to him she made a remark. Here with yo little mannish self"

Smiling as she closed the door on him.

Making her way back to the kitchen, she began putting things to make breakfast. Going over things in her head that she needed to tell the girls while she cooked. Queen heard car doors shut at the same time as her cell phone went off.

"Hello Queen speaking"

"Yo Queen this Teezy, I'm getting low"

"Ok glad you call I'll put you down for the usual"

"Cool, what time do we meet?"

"Give me about two hours"

As she hung up the phone she heard Honey and Sticky coming inside the house. “Moma! Moma!” Sticky shouted all ghetto like.

Walking into the kitchen seeing her Moma cooking serabble eggs, becon, butter cheese grits, hash brown with ham and pancakes. Sticky went and sat at the table, while Honey came around the corner on the phone. “Dang Ma it smells good up in here.” Hanging up the phone then hugging her mother’s neck. Honey looked at everything she was cooking and knew it was going to be a long week.

She took off and sat at the table with Sticky. “Aye Sticky who did you call to come get that car”

“Oh I called Mario from 4th ward, why what’s up?”

“Ok just wanted to know, I’m not trying to get caught up”

“Girl you good, you know I handle business the right way”

“What yall over here talking about” Queen asked as she gave them their plates.

“Nothing but how packed the club was last night” Sticky hurried and spoke while they sat there eating Queen went over the schedule for the week. Starting off with the easy stuff and finishing big.

The girls knew it was going to be some good money made the week plus the money they made from last night. Once they had finished eating, Queen made Sticky and Honey do the dishes, while she got Teezy’s package together. Coming back to the dinning room 15 minutes later, Queen sat a black and green duffle bag with a crown on it on the table.

“Sticky you know the rules pick up and drop off and come straight back”

“Ma I know this already, I been doing this since I was 13”

“I know how long you’ve been doing this but hussy this my money you playing with.”

"Whatever" Sticky said while smacking her teeth.

As she took the back off the table and headed for the door. Queen reached out and popped her upside the head. Honey laughed as she came behind her. Queen popped Honey then stated "Not so funny now is it" then shut the door behind her. Making her way back to her bedroom to get dressed to run her errands.

Sticky: T.H.N

While making her way to the drop off spot, Sticky kept an eye out for some extra money. "It's nothing like having your own"

Sticky thought to herself as she drove up behind the discount make Call. Queen to tell her that she was outside waiting. Queen clicked over and called Teezy. "Aye I'm out back" then hung up the phone on them both. Stepping put side the car then lend up against it while waiting for Teezy to come out the door. Her phone starts to ring "You what up"

"Aye I just cashed out give me an hour then meet me on blud."

"Ok I'll be there"

Soon as she hung up Teezy was walking to the car. Opening up the back door to drop off the duffel bag. Soon as he closed the door Sticky popped the trunk for him to grab the other bag.

"Damn so you antisocial today?"

"Now just trying to get it over with I have other thing to do"

Teezy just looked at her then walked off. Not having time for the bullshit or games he had get back to his money.

Sticky jumped back in the Honda and headed down old Bill cook. Thinking about how she wanted to make more money. And liking the fact that she was good at tricking nigga and robbing them that might be her best move. Thinking how she was going to get

Honey to act right so she could Robb some more of her heavy hitters. Pulling up at the house, she looks around before she got out the car. Grabbing the duffle bag off the back seat then took it inside.

"Mom where you at?"

"I'm in the back, so bring it back here"

Walking to the bed room she see Queen still getting dressed. She dropped the bag off on the bed then walked back out the room. Rushing back out the house Sticky cut across the yard and went inside of her own crib. By passing Honey talking on the phone she went straight to take a shower.

Honey: T.H.N

"Nigga you always talking about beating this pussy up but you stay going to sleep in it"

"Girl that's just because I be tired from working"

"Nigga you aint got no job"

"Girl hustling is hard work"

"Boy just admit that this nookie is to much for you" Honey giggled

"Aye look I'll be back in town in a few days, but I got to go for now."

"You always running from my question but ok I'll see you then baby"

Hanging up the phone as she laid across the sofa. Flipping through the channels, Sticky came back to the living room. "Let's go pick this money up from Mario" stated Sticky as she waited for Honey to roll off the sofa. It had dawned on Sticky that she didn't bring that money form last night inside. She raced out to the car and grabbed the little red bag. Almost running Honey over as she ran back in the house to hide the bag.

"Dang Sticky slow down that money ain't going nowhere"

"Girl I know I just want to put it up"

As they were walking out of the house they saw Queen pulling out of the driveway. "Honey you drive this time" Sticky said as she was walking over to the Camera. Once they were in the car Sticky began to make small talk. Trying to figure out where Honey's head was at about making money. And she knew if Queen could get away with pimping her from time to time, she would most definitely go for what she had in mind. The whole ride to 4th ward Sticky was gassing Honey up. Making little jokes about how they would be tag teaming the game. But Sticky wasn't sure if she was really going for it.

Pulling up at the gas station right next to a set of apartments, Sticky spots Mario posted on the hood of his car. "Come on Honey there he goes right there". Honey put the car in park and they both jumped out. Making their way over to Mario, they heard people yelling and whistling out the car window as they drove by.

Sticky: T.H.N

"Yo what's good bruh, this my sister Honey"

"What it do Jones?"

"So everything was good right?"

"Yeah, I got your money in the car and whenever you come across some shit let me know"

"Ok well check it let me run some things by you and you tell me what you think"

"Ok shoot"

Sticky begin to run a little game plan out to Marion to see what he think and to see if they could make money together. As they went back and forth with ideas, 4th ward slim came pulling.

“Excuse my P and the P is for pimping. Boi Mario, who you got with you?”

Sticky and Honey turned to the side and looked at him, while Mario explained who they were.

“Damn! Sticky and Honey with names and bodies like that, I’ll have the track going crazy”

“The track!! Mario you better get this fool” Sticky stated with a crazy look other face.

“Honey, take a walk with me if you don’t mind.”

Honey smiles at Sticky as she walks off. Sticky shakes her head and goes back to talking to Mario.

Honey: T.H.N

“Baby it’s money to be made out her and you got the right pimp backing you”

“Oh really, so how much money will I be making?”

“See now you crossing the line, you don’t never question me what I say goes”

“Yes daddy” Honey giggled

4th Ward Slim put her in his little Honda with the loud pipes and headed to the track. Beating up her ears with his pimping, he couldn’t believe how easy it was to bag her. As they arrived on Fulton industrial, 4thWard slim pulled into the Mcdonalds parking the car hopping out, Slim made Honey do a full 360° so he could fully check out her body. The high yellow redbone had hazel green eyes, nice juscy titts, long brown hair with blond highlights and slightly bow legged. Standing at 5'5 and weigh no more than 130 pds.

4th Ward Slim knew he had done caught a gold mind. He showed her around, all of the ends and outs. And how other pimps would be pulling up on her trying to get her to jump ship. Before they knew it, they had been out there for hours and it was getting late. Her phone had been blowing up and she didn't even know it. It was in her purse that was in the car. She left out of the hotel room and went back to the car to grab her purse. As she made it back in to the room, Slim was standing in his boxer

"Come on it's time to get broke it"

"I thought I only get it from you went I do something good"

"What I tell you about questioning me "Slim said as he rised his hand as if he was about to hit her. walking over to her Slim grabbed her by her head and pushed her down to make her give him oral sex.

Sticky: T.H.N

Driving up and down Fulton industrial looking for Honey, she finally spots her running down the meter. Cutting through traffic to get to the meter, Sticky let down the window and yell for Honey.

As she drove closer to meet Honey, she saw and heard the Honda coming up behind her. Speeding up then opening the door for Honey to jump in. Hitting the gas and whipping the car around spitting rocks from under the car. Sticky shot 4thWard Slim, a bird as she drove off in the opposite direction. Going in and out of traffic to get a good lead on him.

Honey sat in the passenger laughing and trying to catch her breath. "Bitch what the hell!" Sticky yelled out.

"Girl he was trying to pimp me"

"You knew that was going to happen when you left but why are you running?"

"Oh he tried to make me suck his dick and I bite it, then grabbed his pants and took off out the door."

Honey went on telling Sticky about everything he showed her and how he was talking, as they made the way back home.

Queen B: T.H.N

Arriving at the OLG, Queen pulled one of the waitresses to the side explaining to her what she needed her to do, as she gave her a few dollars. The waitress told Queen to follow her as she took her to be seated. Five minutes later Queen cell went off.

"Hello"

"I'm here, where are you?"

"Ok good, just ask for Gabby and she will seat you"

Tuck asked around for Gabby until she came. Asking no question Gabby told him to follow her. As they walked through the restaurant, Gabby led him to an area that looked like a small conference room. She told him to take a seat.

And handed him a small Walkie Talkie. Tuck looked at the radio with a puzzled look. Gabby walked out the Room and slide the door close. Soon as Gabby gave Queen the thumbs up she pulled out her radio.

Coming across the air wave, Queen told him to state his business. As she listen to him through her ear piece, Queen wrote down notes and direction. When she thought he was about finished, Queen called Gabby over to the table. Handing her a small manila envelope and told her to take it to him and bring it back. Queen waited for Gabby to come back with her envelope then she ordered a meal to go. Giving Tuck time to leave the restaurant, Queen looked over her notes.

Gabby pulled back up with Queen's order then gave her a look as if she wanted in. Queen picked up on the look and smiled at her. "You're not ready for this lifestyle here baby, but I'll keep an open mind for you." Queen stated as she got up from the table. Grabbing her keys out of her purse then headed for the door. Checking her surroundings before she went to her car. Queen wanted to make sure she kept her a low profile.

Queen got inside her car and headed home. Arriving at the house 45 minutes later, she noticed that Honey and Sticky was at the house. She texted Sticky and told her to come over it was something that she needed to talk to her about. Waiting for her to come out the house, she being counting her money.

T.H.N: Sticky

Sticky finished splitting up all of the money, then took Honey her half. Making a cool hundred and ten thousand dollars made Honey eyes get buck. That was the most money she have ever seen or had of her own. Sticky handed her the money and told her to keep her mouth closed. Making haste to get out the house and to make it over to her mom's before she not mad. As she cut across the lawn, Queen flicked the head lights at her.

Sticky turned and begun looking in the car: Queen sat there waving her hand. Sticky walked to the car and got inside. As soon as the door shut, Queen began telling her all the details and the location of the mission. Sitting there for hours to make sure Sticky had it down pack. Knowing that she had her work cut off for her, she took the address down and got out the car. Shooting back inside the house, Sticky grabbed her steak out gear and left back out.

Two hours later, Sticky was arriving in Macon. Parking across the street from her target's house, she grabbed her camera out her bag and began taking pictures. Monitoring the traffic that came and left. Sticky knew she had to come up with a good game plan to hit her target.

Chapter 3

T.H.N: Sticky

Two days later Sticky was back in Macon but this time she had her driver with her. "Yo Q wait here don't move until you see me coming out the house." Sticky told as she got out the car. Making her way across the street, Q sat back in the mustang and watched her. Trying to figure out how she was going to pull this off in a dress. As sticky was walking up to door, it was opening. A slight panic came about but she quickly shook it as she realized that it was only trap traffic.

As they walked by her they all turned their heads trying to check out her Ass. Sticky walked up the three steps and lend on the door. As brown skinned guy stood at the door looking at her. Sticky looked down to check out her body to see if something was out of place. Then looked back up and before she could say a word the guy asked her. "Who are you looking for Cuz?"

"Umm, is there a Neko that stay here."

"Yeah, follow me."

The guy shut the door behind him and Sticky saw the A.K. Posted up on the wall. As the guy led the way and began to shout out Neko's name, Sticky made her move. Jumping on his back and putting him in the choke hold. Wrestling him down to the ground Sticky applied more pressure. Once he was out Sticky quickly reached up her dress and pulled down a small pouch. Unzipping the pouch that was taped to her leg. She pulled out some zippy ties and a small roll of duct tape.

Hurrying to restrain him before any more traffic came to the house. As she was tearing off a piece of duct tape to cover his mouth, she heard someone approaching them.

"Yo Ant what's taking you so long" the deep voice Rowed down the hall as the footsteps got close. Taking the Glock nine out the pouch. and sprinted across the room. Sticky placed her back against the wall and waited for whoever it was, to come around the corner. As the tall dark skinned guy came around the corner, Sticky cocked the 9mm and told him don't move. Thinking to herself "Damn this nigga is bigger than I thought."

Turning around smiling with a mouth full of gold, the guy began to chuckle. "Who sent yo lil fine ass in here to rob me?"

"Don't worry about just get on the ground and I'll be gone in no time"

"Ma you know I can't go out like that, I'm the great Neko baby"

"I know who you are that's why I'm here."

"Look you need to get down with this cripping, I can use a rider like you"

"Enough talking gets on the floor before I shoot"

Still talking shit as he slowly got on the floor. Sticky walked over slowly to make sure Neko was flat on the floor. As she reached for the zipties, while sitting on his back. Neko made slick comments about her having her pussy on his back. Slapping him upside the head and telling him to shut up, as she tried to put his hands inside the zip ties. Neko pushed up off the floor making Sticky slide one way and the gun the other. Both of them went after the gun.

Sticky tried her best to wrestle with the 6'2, 250 pound monster. Neko stopped playing with her and overpowered her. Pinning her down to the floor, Neko climbed on top of her. "I told you lil bitch

I couldn't go out" stated Neko as he let his golds show. Twisting and Turning trying to break loose, all Sticky could think about was getting her hand on that gun. Neko followed her eyes, catching her looking at the gun. Neko took her hands and put them together then reached for the pistol. As he was reaching someone knocked On the door. "Lil bitch you better not say a word" Neko stated as he got ready to climb off of Sticky.

Being able to move her legs, Sticky kneed Neko in the growing and rolled from under him. Grabbing the gun and slapped him across the face with it, spitting his face open. Sticky hurried and grabbed the zip tires and tied him up. Beginning to scream for help as the knocking continued. Sticky hit him again to shut him up, then quickly covered his mouth with tape. As she got off the floor, Ant was coming back around.

As Ant and Neko laid on the floor looking at each other tied up, Sticky ran through the house. Going straight to all of the spots that she was giving, Sticky confiscated everything. As she dropped the duffle bag of weed and money off at the front door, she decided to grab the guns as well. Coming from the back room Sticky tripped over a small Rug. Hurting her toe made her left up the Rug to discover a latch on a small door. Unlocking the latch and opening the door, sticky found bricks of money wrapped in cellophane.

Getting stuck like a deer in the headlights, Sticky was amazed from all the money. Snapping back from the sound of a cell phone going off. Sticky started pulling the bricks of money out of the floor. Then ran back to the bedroom and snatched the quilt off the bed. Placing the money inside the quilt then tied to secure everything. Making her way back to the front door as she stepped over Ant and Neko.

Peeping out the window before she exited the house, making sure the traffic was gone and she could leave freely. Sticky Ran out the house and signal for Q to pull up. As he was pulling up She was Running in and out the house bringing everything to the curve. On her third trip she closed the door behind her, while Q was loading up the mustang. Making her way back to the car, Sticky threw the quilt of money on the back seat then jumped in the car. Q slapped the car in drive and hauled ass.

Drifting around the street corner Q cut it close to hitting a Royal blue box Chevy. The four guys that was in the Chevy turned and looked at the Red Mustang, as it picked up speed going down the street. As Q made his way through the streets and back to the highway. He informed sticky that the blue Chevy was headed back to the house they just left from. "Well that's not our problem now is it, that's why I have the Mustang Kidd as my driver "Sticky Replied in confidence that they was going to get away.

As they hopped on the highway, Sticky let the seat back to relax. While they halved ass down the highway it dawned on Sticky, to text Queen and let her know the mission was complete. The closer they got back to the city the more sticky begin to think about the money. With the notes and direction she was given, the money that was wrapped in Cellophane was unaccented for. It was a free check for them both.

T.H.N: Honey

Hearing knocking at the front door, Honey left out of the bathroom to answer the door. Looking out the peephole at a dozen of Roses, Honey opening the door to be greeted by Gotti. Standing there in shock with Rollers in her hair, Gotti wrapped his arms around her and kissed her on the neck. Honey took him by the hand and led him inside the house.

"Baby why didn't you tell me you were coming!"

"It would be better if I surprised you."

"Nigga you just want to see if you could catch me doing something wrong."

"Come on baby, you know I'm too player for that shit."

"Oh so you a player now."

"Girl don't start and matter of fact come on to this back Room."

"Is that all you want from me Gotti."

"Naw, in a matter of fact I got something to tell you but it can wait for now."

"Shutting the bedroom door, Gotti began undressing Honey. Kissing on her body parts as he removed each piece of clothing Gotti laid her on the bed after taking her panties off. Standing there shirtless with all of his chains on, then quickly dropped his pants. Pulling Honey to the edge of the bed and slowly placed himself inside of her. Gripping the sheets with each stroke that he took, Honey tried her best to hold in her moans.

The deeper his strokes got, the more Honey tried to get away. As Gotti found his groove, she began to losing up.

T.H.N: Queen B

Sitting down looking over everything that Sticky pulled out of the black duffle bag. Queen smiled at the fact that Sticky might be better at robbing then she was. As she separated the different pounds of weed, she reached over and grabbed a roll of money. Tossing the roll to sticky then informing her that she had two small runs for her to do. Shaking her head as she picked up the two duffle bags.

"Umm is there a problem"

"Yeah why Honey don't never make no runs?"

"Because I told you to do it and Honey is not as good as you."

"What's so hard about making drops and picking up money."

"Look if you want to stop making runs then train her on what to look for."

Sticky left out the house as Queen continued to count the money. Grabbing her phone Queen sent out two text too Teezy and Redman letting them know that their pack was on the way. A clean lick for ten pounds and two zips of pills and only sixty thousand in cash. Queen put everything back in the duffle bag and took it to one of the bedrooms. Unlocking one of the four safes, she stacked the money on top of the other stacks. Then opened up one of her rubber bins and placed the weed and pills inside.

Making her way back to the living room, she got a text from an unknown number. Looking confused as she read the text, "I'm watching you" Deleting the text then sitting the phone down on the table. Queen begins to get things set up for the night. Not even giving a second thought about that text, Queen had seen them all before. Getting crazy texts or calls only made her hustle harder. Still feeling like the old her, where she could get you touched no matter where you were.

Receiving a knock on the door had Queen a little edgy but not worried. Grabbing the 357 off of the bar then opened the door. Standing with the pistol on her hip scaring the young female. "Umm is this a bad time?"

"No baby, what do you need?"

"Umm my grandma wants an old English beer and two Newport singles."

"Ok sugar right this way"

Queen took the Old English out the refrigerator, and placed it in a brown paper bag and handed her two Newport's. Putting the money into a small safe above the refrigerator then walked her to the door. As she opened the door she saw Sticky's car still parked in the driveway. Wondering why she hadn't left yet, she went back inside to make a call.

T.H.N: Sticky

"Oh lord its my mom, she is getting on my nerves" Sticky stated to Q as she turned down the radio, "Hello"

"Why haven't you left yet?"

"What do you mean I'm in ThomasVille now"

"Whose car are you in then, because your car's out front"

"I'm with my drive and I'll be back soon"

Hanging up the phone as A.D A.K.A Redman walked up to the car. Sticky got out of the car with the duffle bag this time, because she had too much going on inside of the mustang. Having the trunk full of guns and the back seat with a blanket full of money she couldn't take any chances. Exchanging bags, Redman asked Sticky when she was going to bring Honey back over. And as soon as he asked her that he heard the door shut. Knowing that his baby moma zett had heard him, he gave Sticky some dape and went inside.

Sticky climbed in the back seat, while Q headed back to the Southside. Sticky untied the quilt and begin looking at the faces on the bills. Seeing only one brick with fifties in it, Sticky realized that it wasn't as much money as she though it would be. Dividing the bricks into two palls starting with the five dollar bill, up to the twenty. Then unwrapped the brick Of fifties and split it between the two palls. Concealing her half back inside the blanket, then pushed Q's half on the floor behind his seat.

Sticky jumped back in the front self as Q pulled up in the drive way. Telling him to sit tight until she got back, Sticky took both duffle bags inside. Sitting the bags on the bed then leaving out of the bedroom. Queen begin to make small talk but sticky didn't say a word. She kept walking for the door, hearing Queen coming behind her she speeded up. "Santana Nicole Armwood I know you hear me!" Queen yelled out as Sticky shut the door in her face.

Sticky opened the car door and grabbed the blanket off of the back seat. "Aye keep the straps at your spot until later." Stated Sticky as she closed the car door. Quickly making her way into the house, before Queen or anybody else came out the door. Bumping into Honey as she was creeping out of her bedroom. "Why are you sneaking out of your room?"

"Shh! Gotti done fell asleep in this pussy again."

"Girl whatever you don't have Gotti in your room"

Honey pulled out her phone from her Robe pocket and showed Sticky a picture of Gotti. Shaking her head as she walked off and went to her room. Shutting the door behind her, then tossing the money on the bed. Feeling lucky with the two licks, she threw the money on the bed. Feeling lucky with the two licks she hit, Sticky felt like things could only get better. Unwrapping and counting up her half of the money. Having seventy five thousand plus the five thousand Queen tossed her, Sticky had her a clean eighty bands.

Sticky turned on her long way Sinatra CD and put it on number eight. "Bankroll". And started dancing around the room throwing money in the air.

T.H.N: Honey

"Come on Sticky for real, I told you Gotti was sleeping" Honey yelled out as she beat on Sticky's door. As she stood there banging on the door Gotta came out of the Room. Standing in the doorway in some Armani boxes and all white Gucci Jeans. "Aye come here bae" Gotti said as he extended his hand out at her. Turning around smiling as she walked over to Gotti. Wrapping his arm around her and pulling her inside the room.

Pushing the door up behind them, Gotti begin to tell Honey how he wanted to take her around the world. Honey couldn't believe what she was hearing. She knew Gotti had a lot of groupies, and he told her a while back that he didn't want nothing serious. Not knowing how to take what he was telling her. Honey stopped Gotti and asked him was he serious and why now. Before he could answer the question he interrupted.

Answering his cellphone and within five minutes of the call Gotti's whole attitude changed. As he finished getting dressed with the phone still up to his ear, he lead in and gave Honey a kiss on the cheek. "Bae I'll call you later, " Gotti told her as he walked form the bedroom door. As they walked out the Room Sticky was coming up the hallway. "Damn it's really you, I thought she was lying."

"Naw it's me the one and only"

"So Gotti not trying to be in your business or nothing but Umm….."

Before she could finish her statement Honey stepped in.

"Girl can't you see he is on the phone, get at him next time."

Brushing Sticky off as they walked past her, all she could think about was keeping him from changing his mind. She didn't want her little sister fucking it up for her, with all of them question she was about to ask. As she let Gotti out of the house, she blew him a kiss them motioned for him to call her.

As she walked back inside Struky was standing there waiting on her. "Damn you act like I want that nigga or something."

"Girl don't start with me."

"Yea you right I don't want to mess up your little fancy life."

"Don't get mad because you don't have no one that wants to fly you around the world."

"Whatever I can do that on my own."

Sticky walked off headed back to her Room. While Honey came behind her singing "Flawless" Sticky turned around and gave her an evil look before she shut the door. Honey knocked on her door then took off back down the hallway. Running inside of the bathroom, and cracking the door just enough to peep out. Honey waited a few minutes then did it again. Trying her best to get on Sticky's nerves. But once she didn't come at the second time, Honey decided to jump in the shower.

Chapter 4

T.H.N: Queen

Later that night Queen had done open up shap. She had more business then she could handle at the time. Sanding out a text to Honey and Sticky, telling them that she needed their help A.S.A.P. As she continued cooking up plates and selling beers, the gambling tables Ran themselves. Having some new faces in and out tonight, she needed an extra pair of eyes.

Taking two plates of wings and fries over to the black Jack table. She noticed that one of the players was on the phone. And that was a big No No for her gambling house. As she sat the trades on the tray holders, then politely asked him to turn it off. Walking back towards the kitchen. The front door open. Feeling more comfortable with Sticky and Honey there Queen went and gave them both a hug.

“Ok I need one of you to help me in the kitchen and the other to watch the dor and tables when your not doing nothing.” Queen commented.

“Ok I got you.” Sticky replied.”

Queen Rushed back to the kitchen to pull out the Taplia she had in the grease. Honey walked around battle to table check on everyone, while she was scoping out their pockets for her own benefits. As she walked over to the spades table, a guy that was sitting at the tonk table asked for around of dollar shots. V-lining her way pass the spades table and into the kitchen. Telling Queen what she needed, Queen handed her two hamburger plates and one Fish plate. Telling her to drop them off at the dice game then come back.

As she took the plates over to the dice game, she noticed her ex boyfriend David standing around the table. While the dice Rolled down the padded tablet, Honey dropped the plates off. Trying not to say nothing to him as she placed his plate in front of him. Grasping her hand as he walked off, Honey stopped and turned around slowly. Never really for giving David for breaking her heart she still had love for him because he was her first.

Standing there looking at him as he got closer to her. He lend in and told her that he was sorry and that he still loved her. Giving him a half of a smile then walked off. Knowing that he was full of lies and games, it was hard to resist his charming ways. Walking back inside the kitchen, Queen had the shots ready along with two more plates. Sticky walked into the kitchen and grabbed two beers and asked Queen to make two hot wing plates to go.

Handing her the money then stepping to the side, so Honey could come by with the shots. Stealing a few fires out of the Tray, while waiting for Queen to pour the hot wings in. Popping Sticky on the hand and telling her not to play with people's food as she closed the trayes. Sticky grabbed both plates and took them and the beers back to the front door. As she handed over everything she noticed more traffic was coming up. And almost getting knocked over from the crowd that was coming out of the house.

Sticky swore it was a shift change or something. Greeting all of the new comps. And making sure they all left their guns in the car and their cellphones was off. Sticky let them inside and wished them lock. Getting a call from Q sticky remembered that she was supposed to pick up her half of the guns.

"What's good burh?" Sticky answered

"Nothing really just about to hit this party" Q replied

"Oh yea where at and who throwing it?"

"It's at Creal Park but its for the Southside."

"Ok say no mo I'll be there and don't forget to bring my half"

"I never took them out the trunk."

Sending Honey a text to let her know that she had to take over for a minute, because she needed to make a Run. Honey didn't even respond, she was too busy flirting. Queen had to come out of the kitchen to get her attention. Pulling her back into the kitchen with her Queen whispered good job into her ear. With everybody being drunk and Honey walking around flirting, Queen would get a bigger cut from their losses sending her back out there with a round of shots for the black jack table.

Queen really knew how to work the crowd. Once a table spend amount of money she would send out free shots.

T.H.N: Sticky

Driving down Flat shoals Sticky saw all kind of car parked on the side of the street. The closer she got the more packed it was. Riding through the park looking for Q, she saw a lot of old friends. As stick, was leaving out the park exit she spotted Q walking. Pulling up and picking him up, sticky took him back to his car. Quickly transferring the guns in to her trunk, then parking a car ahead of him.

Walking inside of the park, it was like a big block party. The last time she saw all of these forks was on College Park day. Running into her little cousin ked and seeing how he was all grown up now. She wanted to see what was up with him. Pushing up on him while he was with his crew, he was excited to see her.

"Oh snap what's up big Cuz" Ked shouted out

"Nothing much Cuz I see you done became a young man."

"Yeah I'm all grown up, so you can't call me il ked anymore."

"Oh really!! So what do they call you now?"

"Southside Ked or Ked"

"Well you will always be my lil Ked Cuz" Sticky giggled at him.

Giving her little cousin a hug then walked off. She noticed that Q had done left her. Dj Willie Stroud had the music blaring through the speakers. And everyone was having a good time. Sticky decided to get her Ai drink to lose up, as she moved through the park.

T.H.N: Honey

As the time passed by the house started to thin out. And Honey was making more money then she thought she would. While flirting with a guy her cell phone went off, playing Kevin Gates.

"We are supposed to be in love." Honey knew it was only one person that has that ringtone on her phone. She immediately stopped what she was doing and took the call.

"Hey baby what's up."

"Aye pack your bags we are living as soon as you get to the airport."

"What?! Are you for real?! Oh my god I can't believe this."

"I'll see you when you get to the Airport."

Honey hung up the phone and run inside the kitchen to Queen. Kissing her on the cheek, then telling her that she had to go. Queen stood there with a puzzled look, before she asked her where she was going. But Honey was to excited to even hear. Queen talking to her. As she made her way to the front door, she heard Queen yell at her name.

"Hope Jana Armwood" I know you heard me asking you where you were going. Honey stopped and turned around and said with my boo Gotti and I don't know when I'm coming back love ya" and went out the door.

Running across the lawn and into the house, Honey ran into her room and grabbed her Coach suitcases out of the closet. Filling them up with some of her flies gear. Once she finished packing she called up an Uber, then jumped in the shower to fleshing up.

T.H.N: Queen

Making her last call for alcohol, call before she shut down the kitchen. Everybody was good and tipsy or high from the blunts of Kush that Queen also sold. Queen made sure that everybody was straight. Having all corners of her hustle on lock. Queen went and stood by the spade table, it was the last one going. While standing there she noticed that the same young guy was on his phone.

Queen cleared her throat, catching his attention, then pointed to the door. Getting up shaking his head as he gave her a sight mug mixed with a devilish grin. Queen stood there with her hand on her hip, while still pointing at the door. As he walked by her she followed behind him. Letting him out then locking the door behind him, Queen walked back to the table. They had just finished their last hand.

Everybody stood up and left from the table, while Boobie and cold world counted and split their winnings. Finally getting up from the table, Boobie slid Queen a few extra dollars. Trying his best to win her over. Queen took the money and placed it inside of her bra as she walked them to the door. Boobie continued trying to flirt with

Queen but she wasn't buying it. Telling them to have a nice night as she shut the door.

Walking back though the house straight up, as she picked up both safes out of the kitchen. Dumping all of her money out onto the bed, and counting it up. Making cool out onto the bed, and counting it up. Making a cool 75 hundred, Queen knew that she was going to sleep good tonight. Taking the money and put it in her hidden safe room. Queen made one last security check and turned off all of her lights. Hopping in the shower to relax and fleshing up.

As the hot water hit her body, she began to get an urge to release herself. Slowly rubbing on her clit then speeding up as hse got into it. Taking her finger and sliding inside of her tight pussy. Queen stoked herself while she rubbed and gripped her breast. Letting out soft moans as she reached her peak. Queen cleaned up and jumped out of the shower. Hearing a knock at the door she quickly dried off and threw her robe on.

Walking to the door, Queen tighten the Robe belt, scouring it from opening up peeking out the small window next to the door before opening it. Queen saw a young boy standing there with two dollars in his hand. Opening the door to see what it was that he needed. Queen was in for a Rude awakening. As soon as the door came open, the young boy pulled out a baby 9mm and rushed the door.

Knocking a Queen to ground, then turning around signaling for help. Crawling backwards trying to get away from the door. Queen made a run for it. Trying to get to the 357 that was laying on the kitchen counter. Hearing footsteps and voices behind her. Queen snatched revolver off the counter and started shooting. The young guy and his crew ran and ducked behind the wall. Waiting for her to run out of bullets. With only one bullet left, Queen made a run for the back room.

Running out the kitchen and right into the young boy. Queen shot him right in his chest. The impact knocked the young boy back and on his ass. Queen took back off towards the room, but got clipped up before she could Reach the room. Kicking and screaming trying her best to break free. The guys drugged her back to the living Room. Making comments about fucking her and how petty her pussy was, as the Robe united and opened up.

Sitting Queen in a chair and taped her arms and legs together to restrain her. One of the guys took off to check on their home boy. Seeing him laying there with a whole in his chest brought tears to his eyes.

"Aye wound! We gotta get out of here."

"Who just chill we got this bitch."

"Now wound we got to take the bitch with us and take Spike to the hospital."

"What's wrong with my little brother Chop?"

"I don't think he will make it if we don't leave now."

Leaving Queen in the sit zone took off over to check out Spike. Seeing his little brother laying there like that pissed him off. He Ran back over to Queen and slapped her out of the seat. Telling Chop to go get the car as he pulled spike to the front door. Sitting him up against the wall, then taking back off to search the house. Flipping and knocking over everything that wasn't bolted down.

Finding the rubber bin with the weed and pills in it, Zoe pushed it to the front. Meeting Chop at the front door eh help him put spike on the back seat. Then Run back in to grab Queen and Rushed back at the house. Throwing her into the trunk, while chop stuffed the rubber bin behind the passenger seat. Then they both jumped into the all-black Lincoln and hauled ass. Flying down Old Bill Cook, trying to get as far away from the house as possible.

T.H.N: Sticky

Pulling up into the driveway Sticky noticed that Queen had her door wide open, especially at this time of Wight. Sticky grabbed her gun from under the seat and got out of the car. Putting one into the chancer before she went any farther, then pulled out her phone. Calling Queen cell yelled out "Ma" while walking into the house. Seeing blood on the wall by the door and everything flipped over.

Sticky hung up the phone and placed both hands on the pistol, as she walked through the house. Searching for her moma or a clue to who did this. Sticky took off to the safe Room. Opening up all of the safe to see that the money was still there, threw her for a loop. Scanning the room to see what was out of place. Everything appeared to be there and it was making her frustrated.

Grabbing a few duffle bags out of the closet, then being clearing out all of the safes. It dawned on her while cleaning out the safes, that the rubber bin was gone. Shaking her head in disappointment at herself for slipping her head in disappointment at herself for slipping like that. Sticky hurried and took the duffle bags over to her house. Hinding them all in the addict, Before calling the police.

T.H.N: G

"Gll what's your emergency?"

"Someone just broke into my mother's house and she is missing"

"Ok Ma'am what is your name?"

"Santana Arm wood and Mom's name is Eve Mac Arm wood"

"Ok Ma'am what is your address?"

"3170 old Bill cook lane College Park"

"Ok Ma'am just stay calm, I'm sending a squad car your way."

T.H.N: Sticky

Hanging up the phone with the police, then called Honey. "Come on hope pick up the dawn phone." Not getting an answer after calling back to back, Sticky left her a message. While sitting on the front porch waiting for the police to arrive, she begin trying to remember who was all in the house before she left. Only remembering faces left her at a stand still. Sticky knew she needed more intel to find out who took Queen.

Just when she thought about the hidden cameras, Queen had around the house the police pulled up. Greeting the officer as he approached the porch. Sticky lead him inside to show him how her mother house had been trashed. While officer Patterson checked around the house, he noticed the blood on the wall in two different spot. Beginning to ask more questions about Queen, officer Patterson was interrupted. Sticky had got a call form Honey. Emotionally explaining to Honey what's going on officer Patterson listened very carefully.

As he waited for her to get off the phone, he made a call to the GBT center. A few minutes later sticky got off the phone. Officer Patterson informed her that had called the GBI center and they were on the way. Picking up where he left off at with the question, Sticky felt as if she had make a big mistake involving the police. Not wanting them to find out what all Queen did.

As the time went by the GBI and detective searched the house for evidence. Taking blood samples from the wall and placing them inside Fluorescence bay. As they packed up their things and the sun begins to rise, Sticky was exhausted and frustrated. Looking the door behind them, then begging to straighten up what she could. Hours had pass has Sticky laid across Queen's bed. Hearing a knock at the door startled her.

Grapping her G off the pillow, then tip toed to the front room. Sticky peeked out the side window, really not trying to deal with anybody, she left the little girl standing there. Feeling like it was going to be a long day, she went back to the room and laid down.

Chapter 5

T.H.N: Sticky

Later that morning Sticky was awaken by the combination of her cellphone and knocking. Rolling off the bed grabbing the phone in one hand and the pistol in the other. Silencing the phone as she made her way to the front door. Looking out the peep hole to see an familiar face, Sticky slung the door open with her 9 mm aimed at the guy's head.

"Woe Woe don't shoot, I just came to get my phone"

"Who are you and what time did you leave this house?"

"They call me Bobbie and I left after I won the spades game."

"Ok I remember your face but I don't know where you phone at."

Can you please put the gun down while you talk to me."

"Now, I'm on high alert right now. But leave me you into just in case I find.

As she enter another number to reach him at, Honey was calling the phone back. Shutting the door on Bobbie then peeked back out the side window to watch him walk back down the driveway answering the phone, to hear Honey shoot out." Get this pussy daddy Sticky quickly hang the phone and send her a text.

The text message: Bitch you sitting up here laying on your back while I'm out here trying to find our moma. Don't call me no more, I'll call you when I find out something.

Walking into the room where the security system was hidden at, then opened a double door Chester draw. Rewinding the digital footage to the part where the last man walked out of the house.

Sticky sat there for 30 minutes before it was any action on the tape. Changing the screen from all cameras to Camera one. Where it was a young boy standing at the front door. Watching him rush into the house then waving at some one else. And before she knew it two move guys shot across the camera. Not being able to hear anything, she quickly switched the cameras to ones that was in the house.

Trying to find the right footage, sticky waited until one camera showed her something. But they should nothing but the tables where everybody played at. Getting frustrated at the fact that she couldn't see a thing and that she told Queen a long time ago to change the cameras in the house so she could see more then just the tables. Out of nowhere Sticky shouted out Damn! Remembering that a black car flew by her as she came down old Bill Cook. She switched the cameras back to outside.

Seeing a black Lincoln with no license plate but big chrome wheels backing into the drive way. As she kept watching she saw them put Queen into the trunk. Not knowing if she was dead or alive, Sticky broke down crying. Picking up her phone to call Honey, and to explain everything that she had just found out. Then telling her to stay put until she get everything handle.

Beginning to shake as she balled up her fist out handle.

Beginning to shake a she balled up her fist out of anger. Letting out a loud scream before sending out a SOS text to all of closest friends that are in the streets.

Text: Be on the look out for a black 2016 Lincoln with "24"s or "26"s with me hit back.

Before she could even sit the phone down it was going off. The first text was from her little cousin Ked, letting her know that him and his G's was down for whatever. As the texts rolled in sticky begin to smile, realizing that she had a little pull in the city. Even thou none of her contacts have never ratted on anyone before, their loyalty to her was very respected. Some of it was because of Queen and some it was from the work she put in herself.

Locking up the house then shooting across the lawn to her own crib. Running into change clothes and to gear up with ammo just in cause it was needed. Trying her best to cover up the dick on the drake as she walked to the car. As soon as she stapted up the car a text came to her phone. Reading the text from Q, made her come out the driveway sideways. Racing to get to the Wal-Mart where Q had spotted a black Lincoln.

Coming down Flat shoulder, she picked up the phone to call Q. Making sure he was still there and the Lincoln didn't move. Pulling inside the parking lot Q flicked his lights at her to get her attention. Pulling up next to him as she let down her window, Q pointed to the black Lincoln that was sitting on 24 inch chrome wheels. Getting excited as she go over her plan to Q and not believing how easy it was to catch these fools.

As they sat there waiting to see who was going to get inside of the Lincoln, Sticky realized that the Mustang Kid wasn't in a Mustang.

"Aye Q, who care are you in?"

"Oh this a hot box I got for later."

"Well I need it, I just came up with a new plan."

"Oh lord what now, because me and my brother need a car for tonight."

"Ok you will have one, just fuck with me" Sticky giggled.

Getting out of her car and into the car with Q, Q just shook his head. Running his hands then his Mohawk as a sign of frustration. Sitting back in the seat and beginning to go over the new plans, until she spotted a older lady and child pushing a cart to the car. Stopping in mid of the conversation to jump out the car. Sticky speed walked over to the car, while the lady and little girl placed the grocery in the trunk.

Slowly pulling out the drake, until she got close enough to hit the lady in the back of the head. Laying her down inside the trunk as she snatched her purse off her arm. Closing the trunk and ran to grab the little girl, Q pulled up with the trunk open. Sticky stuffed the little girl in the trunk and Ran back to the Lincoln. With not a lot of people on their side sticky came out the parking lot flying. Q was right behind her cutting through traffic.

Hearing a phone going off, sticky patted herself down trying to find her phone. Once she pulled it out she noticed that it wasn't her. Still hearing ringing she grabbed the purse and dumped it out. picking up the iPhone 8 to see who was calling, It read "Zoe". Letting it ring as she called her little Couse back to see if he duck off spot. Not getting an answer she hung up and called Q.

"Hello"

"Hey you got a spot we can go to?"

Pausing for a second then answer "Yea follow me."

Q switched lines then jumped in front of sticky to lead the way. Within five minutes they were pulling up on old Madison Pl. in College Park. Backing both cars into the drive way, a brown skinned bald headed guy walked out the garage. Q had done jumped at the car to greet the guy, then waved for Sticky to get out the car.

"Yo Sticky this Nino, Nino this Sticky" Q said introducing them favor to each other. Giving each other the look to see if they could trust each other while throwing their heads back to say what's up.

"So what are we doing here Q" Nino asked.

"Shidd bruh you need to be talking to her" Q replied

"So what the move is shawty."

Sticky popped the trunk to show him the lady laying there. Nino grinned and looked back over at Sticky, then told her to hey him get her out the car. Putting a black pillow case over her head, then taking her out of the trunk. As they carried her through the house and out the back door. The lady being to come back too, panicking from seeing nothing but black and being in the air. She begun calling out for the little girl that was with her.

Placing her into the chair and begin taping her arms and legs to it. "This is where all magic happens at" Nino said as he tossed sticky and Q a mask and gloves. Remembering that he had the little girl in his trunk, Q took off back to his car. Opening up the trunk to see the little girl laying there still, made Q panic. Raching in to check her pulse to realize that she was only sleeping. Picking her up and taking her inside the house to lay her on the sofa.

As he entered back into the shed, Sticky was going across the lady's face with some brass knuckles. "Tell me what you know batches" Sticky yelled as she hit her again. Spitting blood on the floor that was covered in a thick plastic, just like the walls. "I don't know your momma or who Robbed her, I swear." The lady cried out hoping that she didn't Get hit again. Hitting her a few more times, to let her think about what's going on while she ran off to grab the phone out the car. On the way back through the house, Sticky noticed the little girl laying on the couch.

Scooping her off the couch and taking her back to the shed with her. Taping her arms and legs together then put a small piece over her mouth. Pulling out the cellphone to call Zoe back. As soon as he answered, Sticky held the phone close to the Haely's mouth. Hitting her up side the head making her scream out help. Zoe begin to asked who was playing games and where was his mother. Sticky hung up the phone and took a picture. Sending him the picture then waited for him to call back.

Not a minute went by before he was calling back. Nino answer the phone and got straight to the point. Being that he had did this before, Sticky took the back seat and let him handle business. While the was going back and forward with him, Sticky was going through her purse. Pulling out her ID and read the address off to Q to see if he knew where it was. Not knowing where the address was, Q shook his head with a confused look on his face while telling her no. Hearing Nino set up a meeting arrangement for that night, Sticky brain went to turning.

Calling up her little cousin to set up her own little Raid.

"Listen and listen good"

"Ok Cuz what is it."

"Look I'm about to text you this address and I need you and the whole crew to ran through the house. Don't spare nothing, if you see your Auntie bring her back to me. And if no one is in the house take what you want, but make sure you leave no evidence that yall was there.

"Ok big Cuz I got you. But what time do you want me to go over there?"

"I'll text you 15 minutes before we head to our little arrangement."

"Ok say no more."

As she hung up the phone with ked, she begin to think about her next move. Knowing that she couldn't come half stepping just in case things got out of hand, she strolled through her phone. Coming across a old friend that though her a lot about the street just like her mother. Sticky walked out the room and gave him a call.

"Yo who dis?"

"John-John stop acting like you don't know my number"

"Hold on…oh Sticky what's up? I was in the middle of doing some homework."

"Oh well I'm glad that I got you while your in that mind frame."

"What's up what made you call?"

"Look I need your help, somebody broke into my momma's house and kidnapped her. And they are holding her for money and I'm going to meet them tonight."

"Say no mo, you know I got your back. She as my second momma, but you still owe me."

"Can we talk about that when I come get you?"

"Shidd you know my niggas coming with me so its whatever"

"Ok I'll call you when I'[m on the way."

Hanging up the phone as she entered back into the shed. Nino asked her if she had everything wrapped up, as he plugged up his hand drill. Sticky looked at him with a puzzled looked on her face, wondering what he was about to do.

"Yeah everything is set on my end but I need to know its cool to leave them here."

"OH yeah its cool, G-body you better tell her whoever enter here for interrogation don't leave back out. We set examples around here, been doing this since Hollywood Court day."

"Ok big bruh we know the stories no need to go down memory lane" Q jumped into stop Nino before he got into his story.

Laughing as he pulled his mask back over his face and started up the drill. Walking over to the lady and placing the drill up to her head, then pulling the botton to rib it up. Frighten form the sound of the drill, the lady begun wiggle to rib it up. Frighten form the sound of the drill, the lady begun wiggle around in the chair. Trying her best to get free but realizing that its no way out, she just started crying.

"So Ms. Adam or would you like he to call you peaches? Well it don't matter you gone answer to whatever I call you. Now you gone tell me everything that I need to know and if I feel like you lying you and the kid gets it."

As Nino started his interrogation Q let his self out. He never could watch Nino work his magic, he just knew that he got, the job done. Sticky was gang for whatever to get what she needed to find her mother. Taking notes and sucking up information, Sticky felt as if she was winning for the moment. The more he tortured her the move into she came up with. But non of it really told where Queen was at. Getting frustrated from not hearing what she wanted to hear, Sticky push Nino to the side.

Slapping Peaches with the back end of her gun, Then grabbed and shook her while asking where was her mother. Spamming out beating her repeatedly, then turning to the kid and begin kicking her as she laid there tied up. Nino sat back to watch her release her anger but the more anger she released the more excited Nino got. He rolled a small cart with six battery's connected together and a set of jumper cables. Hooking one side to the batteries then tapped the other side to create a spark. Before hooking peaches up to the batteries, Nino told Sticky to fill up a bucket with water.

Placing Peaches feet inside the bucket water giving her one last chance to talk, before hitting her with the jumper cables. Peaches cried out.

"I have told you everything that I know." Nino hit her with the jumper cables. Sending electricity through her body for five minutes at a time. Making blood ooze out of the wholes that he had made with the drill. Pausing to take off the pillow case, so she could see what next. Hooking the jumper cable to the little girl until she almost passed out, brought more pain and tears to her eyes. As the child laid there in pain caring, Nino told peaches that he was going to give her time to think.

Tapping her mouth back up and covering her head before they left out the shed. No was Famished form all of the interrogation and was ready to eat. Trying to get Sticky to run him up the road to the hot wing stand. Sticky told him to get in, but not informing that she was going to give him the car. Sticky went right back to Wal-Mart so she could get her car. Hopping out of the car while telling Nino to keep his phone on.

Sticky jumped in her car then told him that the car was all his until later. Giving no exposition to what she just said before pulling off. Nino just laughed as he slide over to the driver seat. Knowing that this, he just let her have her way. Sticky on the other hand was planning her next move.

Talking to herself as she headed to the meeting location for the night. Riding dawn Flint River then hoping on to Taylor Rides Counting out the clock off Roads that she could put at car on, before she jumped on to Thomas Rd. As she arrived at Independence Park she realized that it was a one way in and out. Park. "They could work to my advantage" Sticky thought to herself as she continued to scan the area. Looking at the small wooded area behind the baseball field, Knowing that it was a good but obvious spot for an ambush.

Taking another good look around Sticky seen all she needed to see. Leaving back out the Park Stick's phone goes off. Realizing who it was by the ring tone she quickly answered.

"What do you want Honey?"

"I'm glad to talk to you to, I just wanted to let you know that I'm home."

"I thought I told you to stay put until I handle things."

"I know, but I caught Gotti coming out another bitches room that was two door down form us."

"Uh! Well you know all chicken heads like dope boys and I told you don't get caught up in his smooth talking."

"Girl I ain't no damn Chicken head, I thought what we had was real"

"Well you can tell me all about it while I'm driving home"

Chapter 6

T.H.N: Haitian Eddie

Walking up to a chair half beaten. Haitian Eddie laughed out.

"I finally got yo ass after all these years." In his strong Haitian accent Picking up a black leather belt with metal balls hanging from the end of it, and slapped Queen across the face. Slowly torturing her each time he comes to the back for supplies. But trying his best not to make too much noise so the other restaurant wouldn't hear them.

Making Queen regret that she crossed him for some Asians, and left him for dead. Each time he looked at her it brought back good and bad memories. Just so happen the vengeance that he had for her, made the bad memories stick out move, them the good. sitting there hopelessly Queen still tried to talk her way out of the situation.

"Eddie it wasn't meant to go down like that."

"No! No! Queen your not going to talk your way out of this."

"Eddie I'm not trying to do that I just want to tell you what happen and why things went wrong."

"Ok you can tell me but your still going to die."

"Well if you're going to kill me its no need to tell you how the Asians are moving heroin."

"Don't play with me you fucking bomb cot! Tell me what you know and I'll set you free once I make it back."

"Eddie tell that to someone that don't know you, you must forgot we dated for six years. I know how you operate"

Looking at her with a look that would kill her if looks could kill, before slapping her with his huge hard hand. His hands looked like some thick leather with a sandpaper or concrete coating. Queen dropped her head to spit out a tooth mixed with blood.

Eddie grabbed three small boxes of season before walking back out of the storage shed. As he placed the boxes on the counter to open his cell phone went off.

"Wassie Rude boy?!"

"Bad news! Whoever that lady was that you had me and the crew go get, somebody want her back."

"Fuck em we don't do bomba clot negotiating"

"But they have Moma and Ne Ne"

"No! No! No! Don't know bomba clot body try my me, find him and kill him I will handle my and."

Hanging up the phone in Zoe's face as he turned around slapping the boxes off the counter. You would have swore you just seen the devil how red he turned. Storming back to the shed Kicking Queen and the chair to the floor. Squatting over Queen as he lifted her up just enough to shake her around. Questioning her about the nigga she had looking for her. Not knowing if he was in his feeling or what Queen just looked at him. Making him murder by the minute.

Dropping Queen back to the floor then began kicking and stomping her in the chest and stomach. As she begin to cough up blood, Eddie stopped kicking her and asked her once again "Who do you have looking for you?"

"Nobody I swear."

"You have some little bottle boy out there looking for you, so stop bomb clot lying?

Eddie I know nothing about nothing I been here since you punk ass son and his homeboy broke into my house." Before he could make his next move he was interrupted. Having one of his

Zoe Pound brothers stick their head inside the shed to call him out. Queen laid there thinking to herself on how she was going to get word out to sticky or just break free from her crazy ex's custody.

T.H.N: Sticky

Jumping up from the sofa in realization of the time, Sticky knew she had to get everything in position. Catching Honey up on everything and also finding out what happen to her. Sticky know she had her hands full with trying to fill her mom's shoe. Grabbing her phone off the couch to call her little cousin.

"What's Making?"

"It's time to make that move, but don't go alone and don't be slipping."

"I got you cuz, I got my niggas Bama 4, Migo tom, and laleel we gone get the job done."

"Ok well here is the address again, just to make sure everything is right."

Texting him the address while she gather all of the things she was taking with her. Honey sat there looking at Sticky trying to figure out how was her little sister going to pull this off by herself. As Sticky headed for the door Honey yelled at "wait." Stopping in her tracks sticky turned around "What's up Honey I'm on a time flame." Rushing to the door gust to tell her to be safe and that she loved her.

"Girl you could have just yelled that out, I thought you was about to come with me" Sticky replied.

"Now boo somebody got to stay back to call the cops if thing don't go right."

"Yeah you right, if I don't call you an hour after I text you then call"

"Ok well knock em dead Little sis."

Sticky just shook her head as she climbed inside of her car. Knowing that Honey don't have a violent bone in her body, makes her wonder who genes she came from. Wasting no time trying to get to Riverdale before John, John got into the streets doing other thing feeling and knowing that he was the best and only chance she had to having the upper hand in this situation. Driving through the Cherry Hill subdivision behind the McDonalds, her phone goes off. Thinking that it was John-John calling to either cause her out or to tell her that he not at the spot. Looking at the phone to see who it was realizing that it was him, it was Teezy.

"Hello"

"Damn you are a hard person to catch up with"

"I got a lot going on right now, but what's good?"

"Shied one of my loco's over heard shit about your mom and they told me, so that's why I called."

"Something about a restaurant called Chief Rob's, that's all they could make out"

"OK well that don't ring a bell as of now but if you find out more hit me up"

"That's what's up and another thing, A nigga need to re-up are you still holding it down "Yeah we still doing a little something call Honey and tell her what you want."

Pulling up at the small white house to see John, John and Kebo Gotti standing there talking. While the party was going on inside the house. Sticky got out the car and walked over to see if he was ready.

"What's up baby girl you ready?"

"Yeah I'm ready and why didn't you tell me that yall was throwing a party"

"Oh we aint throwing no party, girl you know how the squad move."

"Yeah Sticky you done been around us long enough to know what we do and by the way where is that fine ass sister of your." Kebo added

"She at home I guess, hell ain't no telling with her."

"Tell her she need to get at me, I'll catch yall later I got hit the studio."

Kebo dapped John-John up before walking off to his gray Durango. John-John ran to the front door and told everybody to load up. "Aye Trez, Mechaz, Sambo, Gregg, Malik, Fish sacle, Cap nad Lile. Need yall to drive, everybody else just load up in a car" John-John yelled out while putting his MP.5 HK on the passenger side of Sticky's car. Having enough artillery to be an small army and to catch life in the feds. Sticky all most wanted to rethink her plan. Flicking the lights to see if everyone was ready to ride, they all blew their horn.

As they begun to pull off, they hear some beating on the trunk. Sticky stopped the car and Panama jumped in the back seat.

"I'm gone ride with yall two" Panama said as he closed the door. Taking back off Sticky noticed that everybody had on all black. And that wasn't usual for them niggas, They use to handle business in whatever they had on. Most of the time they would try to be fresh because they would be coming from a club or going to one.

Catching John-John looking at her made her smile. Feeling like the old days when she would have to pick him up from running from the cops or from hitting licks. Trying to make small talk so she wouldn't get caught up in her old feeling. She begin telling him what she knew about the nigga they was going to meet.

T.H.N: Ked G

Sitting behind the wheel two houses down form the target. Ked told Bama to get a raw cone ready for them. For when they got back, watching the hose for a good forty-five minutes before realizing that no one was home. Everybody got out the car and walked down to the hose. Acting if they belonged their ked and Bama walked to the back of the house. Finding a door that could have been connected to the garage or just a closet. Bama tried the door knob before kicking it in.

As soon as the door went flying open ked and Bama went right behind it. Using the light from the side of the house to find a light switch, with pistol drawn and ready to shoot. Ked found a switch inside a small hallway. Hitting the light to see where they were at. "Damn we are in somebody's bedroom." Bama said as he moved the bed on wheels out the way. Hearing voices coming up behind him, he signaled for ked to hit the lights.

As the voices entered the room, Ked turned the lights back on him and Bama was ready for a shoot out, but it was only Migo Tom and Laleel.

"Man yall niggas was about to be some dead niggas creeping up on us like that" Ked stay.

"Bruh yall was taking too long we to open the front door" Migo Tom replied

"Fuck it we back here now" Laleel said as he opened the other door. Walking into the dark house, they all stuck together and swept the bottom range. Separating as they made it up stairs. Ked called Sticky to inform her that no one was there and it smelled like some good gas. As he continued giving her the run down, he stumbled across a bag.

T.H.N: Sticky

"What's up CUZ what did you find?"

"Its one of them duffle bag that auntie be putting her work in"

Ok well Keep looking its something that's going to give us her location and remember what I said."

"I know don't get caught and whatever we take its ours."

"Ok well took I got to go call me later."

Getting closer to the park Sticky asked John-John to have a car parked on the side street for back up. Calling up everyone to see who was the last car and to have them post up for enforcement. As they entered the park John-John alertness shot to high, scanning the area for anything that wasn't right. Being great street nigga and a even better Robber, this was his second nature. Arriving at the back of the park, Sticky parked her car facing the exit. Everyone stepped outside of the cars and looked around, trying to figure out what's going on.

"Goddamn! Where then niggas at John-John" Trez yelled out.

"Shid bruh they coming but I need yall to spread out and make it look like its just her here."

"So what we need to move the cars?"

"Yeah duck the cars off and come post up in the woods."

Ready to get into some gangsta shit they all was kind of let down because they were thinking that it was just going to pop off as soon as they got there. Climbing back into the car to relocate while Sticky made her call to Nino.

"Yo Nino I'm here, but I don't see old boy."

"Ok give me a second I'm about to call him on 3 way so you can hear for yourself.

"Ok cool I'll just press a button to let you know that I'm on line."

"While waiting for Nino to click back over, Sticky started o remains about how John-John use to put it down. Looking at him standing there in all black with his broad shoulders and juicy lips with his pistol in hand. Hearing Nino click back in she pushed a button then put her phone on mute.

"Aye my nigga where you at? I'm here with the cash as we discuss."

"Alight bottle boy I'll be there in two minutes."

"Aye what do you mean you'll be there where the fuck is Queen at?"

"I got her you bomba clot" Zoe said as he hung up the phone.

"Hello! Hello! Yo Sticky you still there?"

"Yeah I'm here, I guess I'll hit you up once this is over."

"Just get at me"

Hanging up the phone then pounded her, first together out of anger. Feeling played from how he just handle her, but knowing it wasn't much that she could do at the time. John-John pushed up on Sticky to see what's was up. As she begin explaining to him they heard Leaves and branches being stepped on. Quickly grabbing their strips and aiming at the woods. Waiting to see who was about to come out, self yelled out bruh you don't want to do that." Laughing at the recognition of the voice John-John lowered his gun.

"Say John-John we got company and they not with us" Panama yelled Turning around to get a look at the car as he told everyone to take their places. Him and Panama jumped back inside. Sticky car and turned off the door light to make the car dark inside. As

Sticky stood in front of her head lights waiting for the car to arrive, John-John and Panama checked their guns to make sure they was ready. As they put one inside the chamber, John-John looked up at Sticky standing there. He begin to think about how fine she was and realized that she has gotten even sexier.

"Aye bruh you know we gone make the news shooting we have been in" John-John replied.

As the car approached they lined up in front of Sticky's car. with the head lights shining on bright to see who she had with her. Peeping the move and quickly turning her lights on high to do the same thing. But with both sets of lights on high made it hard for either of them to see in each others car. As Zoe stepped out of the car Sticky walked to meet him half way.

"See bruh that nigga think he slick trying to shine his lights inside the car, but I'm on to all that bullshit." John-John told Panama as they sat back waiting for sticky to signal for him to bring the duffle bag.

Standing there face to face with the nigga that robbed and kidnap her momma. It was taking everything in her not to hit him or pull out her 9mm from behind her back. Staring into his eyes waiting for him to break the silence, Sticky cold sense a small discomfort coming from Zoe. Either he was intimidated by her boldness or something was wrong on his end, Sticky couldn't Put a finger on it right of the top. Breaking the silence by speaking first and asking his name to make sure he was her guy.

"So you are the guy that had the nuts to kidnap my moma?"

"Yeah you can say"

"Umm so where is she?"

"Do you have the money?"

"So this is how this going to go"

"What do you mean I just wanted to make sure you had the money"

"Yeah I got it but do you have my momma?"

"Yeah I got her, she's in the car."

"Ok then lets get this over with bring her out and I'll get the money"

"Not so fast, you got something else that belong to me."

"And what's that?"

"Come on bitch don't play dumb with me, where the fuck is my Momma at?"

"Oh yea I still do got that bitch don't I" Sticky laughed

Making Zoe furies by laughing in his face about having his mother. He turned as if he was about to walk off and turned back around to smack Sticky to the ground. Pulling his pistol off his hip aiming it at Sticky, as he aggressively ask about the where about of his mother. Sticky continued to laugh as she made her way off the ground. Looking back at the car to signal for them to make their move.

"Bitch you got a lot of nerves or just crazy as hell to come out here by yourself. Now lets walk to get this money."

As they begun walking towards the car John-John open the door. Climbing out the car as he waved the duffle bag in the air.

"Throw the bag batting boy." Zoe yelled out at John-John trying to stop him from getting any closer. Tossing the bag mid-way to give Sticky time to Run to the car before he could pick up the money. As soon he let her go, John-John yelled out squad up. Everybody came out of the woods cocking their guns. Letting him know that they meant business. John-John reached back inside the car and grabbed his MP.5 HK. Walking closer and closer to Zoe as her made him get his knees with his hands behind his head.

"Aye my nigga where fuck my momma at and I aint asking nicely."

"She is with my...."

Before he could finish his statement, his car door opened and gunshots was fired. Everybody took their aim off of Zoe went to shooting at everyone and continuing laying down cover for him, he Zippy tied Zoe hands behind his back and drug him to the car. Getting Panama to help him throw the body in the trunk, so he could finish hog tying his feet to his hands. As they closed the trunk they noticed the whole squad was running back through the woods. Rushing Panama and Sticky back inside the car as he ran over to Zoe's car.

Making sure whoever it was he had with him was dead. Waving for Sticky to pull up as he begin making his way back to her. Jumping inside the car smiling as he lined to the back seat to dap up Panama. "Man these sucker know we don't play." Turning around looking at Sticky as she sat behind the wheel shaking her head. Seeing the blood on her lips, made him feel some type of way. But he knew he only did as he was asked, so he just wiped the blood off her lips as she drove.

Making their way out of the park John-John cell went off. "What up bruh"

"Shied yall good?"

"Yeah meet us back at the spot"

As he hung up the phone he sat back in the seat to enjoy the ride as he thought about his next move.

Chapter 7

THN: Ked G

"Oh shit!" Ked shouted as he walked into a small storage room full of bales of weed. Knowing this was going to put them so far ahead of the game, Ked began cleaning out the storage room. Tossing bale after bale at Bama's feet. Standing there looking like a dear caught in headlights, Bama had done forgot all about what he was there for.

"Bama! What are you doing just standing there looking like a young Teddy Pendergrass?! Man we gotta get this shit out of here." Ked stated as he tossed the last bale out of storage.

Hearing a lot of noise coming from down stairs, made them both drop the bales that they had and case down the steps. Seeing Migo Tom and Lateel pulling guns from the closet under the stairwell, made a light go off inside of Bama and Kid's head. Looking over at each other then smiling signifying that they was on the same page."

"Aye I'm about to check up stairs for a safe or just some money" Bama stated as he took back off upstairs.

"Say Laleel go pull the car up so we can load up."

"Ok bruh say no more I'm on it."

"Aye Tom put the guns by the door and help Laleel load them up when he comes back.

Taking back off upstairs bombing into Bama, "Damn Foolie you icy ain't you" laughed as he checked at Bama's new jewelry. As he started rolling bales of weed down the steps, Bama informed him that there was no safe or money in the house. Not sounding right to

Ked, made him paused for a second. Feeling like it should be some money somewhere in this big house, he just shrugged his shoulders and kept tossing the bales down the steps.

Bama hopped over the weed that was paling up on the steps and began slinging them down the rest of the stairs. Migo tom walked back in from taking the guns to the car and let out a loud "Damn! We Gone need one of my momma's moving trucks for all that weed." Wasting no time to load up the 2009 Audi, they realized that the guns and weed wouldn't fit in the trunk.

"Aye bruh it's a car in the garage."

"Good looking Laleel, shred everybody, search for some keys."

Everybody disbursed through the house looking for a set of keys. Knocking and flipping over everything that wasn't too heavy to move. Spending the next 5 to 10 minute looking for the keys made Ked a little thirsty. Walking into the kitchen heading straight for the refrigerator. Opening it up to scan the shelves to see what all they had in there. Spotting a six pack of pineapple Fanta sitting behind a gallon of milk and a pot of curry chicken.

Pushing the pot and milk to the side to pull out the six pack. Popping the top and taking him one to the head. As he quenched his thirst he almost choked from the excitement of finding the keys. Seeing them just sitting hanging from a Key Rack made him feel a little funny. Out of all places" Ked thought to himself as he walked over and took the keys off the Key Rack. As he entered the garage he spotted the SUV hiding under a car over. Quickly snatch off the car cover to see what he was about to hop in.

Seeing a 2016 Candy Purple Yukon Denali on some 30 inch Asante, unlocking the doors and hopping in on some all-white leather seat with purple stitches. Gripping the wood grain as he made himself comfortable. Hitting the garage button to let up the garage as he started up the truck. Damn never jumping out the car from the sound system, he hurried and pulled the truck out of the garage. Bama, Laleel and Migo Tom ran out the house. Ked jumped out of the truck and went to Milly Rocking on em.

"Oow shit boy that bitch clean, but nigga we got to go" Bama said as he took off back inside to grabs the bales of weed. Ked opened the duel doors and saw six 15 inch L7 subs with 3 A6-2800.10 amps. Tossing bale after bale right on top of the subs.

Not having enough room for the last two bales they stuffed them on the back seat of the Audi. Everyone pick a vehicle to get in and hauled ass. Leaving the doors open and lights on in the house, Ked and Bama both laughed at how they had just trashed the house.

"Shid bruh I need to set up some plays."

"Hell yeah I'm about to call my nigga Gino from New Orleans I know he will cop something."

"Shiid I need to hit my cuz up to, to let her know we finished and if she want a little something for putting us on this nice lick."

Changing the way he drove so it would bring no unnecessary heat to the car, as he rode the streets of Clayton County.

T.H.N: Haitian Eddie

"Daman baby after all these years you still know how to get this kitty wet don't you?"

"Eve Mac I'm not falling for your little seducing games this time."

"Eddie you know I wouldn't try that with you. Better yet I'm going to tell you about these Asians so you can get some get back and do whatever you want with me because I'm tired of sitting here."

"Yeah that's your best bet, but for now you gotta hold tight and let me close up shop."

Seeing a devilish grin come upon his face made Queen even more worried. Dealing with him all them years, she knew when he was about to do something stupid. Forty five minutes later Eddie was untying Queen from the chair and retying her hands to each other. Helping her out the chair and walking her to the car with her hands covered. Placing Queen inside the maroon BMW, then quickly sprinted to the other side.

As he pulled out of the parking lot he advised Queen that she needed to start talking. Pulling out the parking lot Queen begin talking.

Only telling Eddie what she wanted him to know. Keeping a few key pointers in the tuck for insurance. Forty minutes later arriving at the house, Eddie sat in the car beating his hands against the steering wheel out of anger. Seeing his garage door open and all the lights on inside his house, he knew he had been hit. Reaching under his seat to pull at his 40 caliber, then climbed out the car and escorted Queen inside the house.

Gripping Queen by the arm as he guided her through the house. Checking all of his spots for his money, weed and guns. Knowing that the weed would be the first thing to go he didn't feel so bad. Getting it by the truck load when needed he knew he really didn't have to sweat it, as long as he had the money for it. Having the classic safe behind a picture, saved him from taking that loss.

"Damn Eddie yo son got you to huh?"

"My step son wouldn't do this me, I'm too good to him."

"Well this damn show look like how my house was when you send them at me."

Nawl that shit ain't gone work Eve Mae, and I owe you for shooting my son Spike."

"I thought that little baster looked like you but I couldn't really tell I was in a heated moment."

Letting out a little chuckle before back handing Queen. Knocking her over the couch then Kaped over it behind her. Choking her while sitting on her chest, his phone went off. "You saved by the phone. You were always lucky" Eddie said as he stopped up to answer the phone.

"Hu assie who dis?"

"Look here you got something of mine and I got something of yours and I don't' have time for smaller talk. So let Queen go and I'll let your boy live."

"I don't take orders form nobody, shit!"

Hanging up the phone to chase after Queen. After seeing her chance to make her move Queen was headed for the front door. Slightly jarring the door before Eddie pulled back inside the house and closed the door. "I see you are still quick on your feet" Eddie stated as he picked Queen up and placed her on his shoulder. Taking her back up the small flight of stair and tossed her back on the sofa. Pasting back in forward contemplating on how he was going to deal with all this mess.

Stopping in the middle of the floor looking at Queen sitting on the sofa. "Come on lets go" Eddie said as he snatched her off the couch. Taking Queen up stairs to his bedroom to grab two huge duffle bags and one suitcase. Filling the suitcase with clothes then moved everything to the hallway. Removing the old picture of Zoe and spike form when he was a baby off the wall to get to his build in safe. Empting out the safe into the two duffle bags. Zipping them up and tossing them across his shoulders, as he made Queen tote the suitcase.

Making their way downstairs and out the front door to the car. Putting the suitcase on the back seat and the duffle bags in the trunk. Queen made another attempt to run for it, cutting across the yard screaming for help. Eddie shot behind her, scooping Queen off her feet and covered her mouth with his other hand. Totting her back across the yard and placed her inside the trunk. Security her form making any more escape attempts. Headed down the road trying to find the nearest hotel.

T.H.N: Honey

"Teezy I didn't know you was this smart, why are you in the streets?"

"Shid everybody got on eat some kid of why and a 9 to 5 is to slow for me."

"Aye not trying to be funny but what are you?"

"Girl what you mean what I'm I! I'm a grown as man"

"Boy you so silly I know that but I mean your not fully black so what are you?"

"Oh why you didn't just say that, I'm Black and Asain"

"Oooh I bet we would make a pretty baby"

"It's only one way to find out, your place or mine"

"Hell why not on the back seat?"

"If that's where you want it then that's cool"

Moving from the front seat to the back, Teezy wasted no time. Kissing Honey all on her neck as he stuck his hand down her pants. Rubbing on her clit as he slowly slide his index finger inside of her. Feeling the wet sentsation of her pussy made Teezy pull his hand out her pants and inbotton them all the way. Sliding her pants and panties down as he position hisself to penetrate her. pulling Honey closer as he slowly place himself inside of her. taking a few strokes before he was stopped. Honey searched for her cell phone, trying not to miss the call.

"Hello"

"Aye where you at?"

"Umm I'm still with Teezy"

"Bitch you need to get home right now, our lil cousin Ked is about to drop off something"

"Why you can't meet up with him? I'm trying to get my Rocks off"

"That's what's wrong with you, you always somewhere with your legs open like a little hoe."

"Whatever I'm on my way"

Hanging up the phone while pushing Teezy back so she could pull up her pants. Sitting there with a puzzled look on his face, he knew and felt as if he had to at least get a quickie in.

"So you just going to stop me just like that?"

"Family come first this time around but we'll catch up"

"Damn so you just gone leave yo boy like this?"

"Yeah for now, it will only make it better the next time"

"Hell naw that's some bullshit cuz, just let nigga get five minutes"

"How about something to make you think about me"

Climbing out of the car then lean back inside to grab Teezy by the click. Placing her mouth tightly around him as she moved her head up And down. As she came back up to the tip, she gave his penis a kiss then stood up to shut the door. Turning around to get inside her car, Honey looked back at Teezy and smiled. Knowing that she left him craving for more made her little excited. Loving to be able to tease a man and to get away with it.

Driving off headed for the house, Honey couldn't stop thinking about how cute Teezy was to her. having a thing for hustlers or niggas with money, she wondered if he was a keeper. As she turned on to old Bill Cook he phone went off. A text form Sticky, telling her to call her once Ked made it to the house. Shaking her head out of frustration, feeling as if Sticky didn't trust in her to handle business. Dropping the phone in her lap as she pulled inside of the drive way.

"I'm show her that I'm just as good as she is with this street shit" Honey said to her self as entered inside the house. Soon as she shut the door and locked it her phone went off. Scaring the shit out of her. As she pulled the phone out of her back pocked, she let out a little giggle" Who am I kidding".

"What's up lil cousin?"

"What's up foolie I'm out side"

"Damn ok I just walked in the house"

"Aye cuz let up the garage for me"

"Ok give me a secong"

While Honey made her way to open the garage, she begins to hear music playing. As she let up the garage door she had seen purple Deanli backing into the driveway. Once the door way up Ked and Bama jumped out the truck. Future ad Darake "Big Rings" song was palying through the speakers. As they open the back doors to the SUV, Bama and Honey locked eyes. "Aye cuz! Honey!"

Snapping out of her little daze from the sound of her name begin called

"Oh what's up Cuz I just had a moment" Honey giggled

"Aye where to you want us to put this?"

"All of it?"

"Naw we just dropping off four of them"

"Ok well let me make some room over here for yall"

Ked waved for Migo Tom and Laleel to come help unload the four bale. As they ran up the driveway Ked and Bama had done grabbed one bale already. Seeing Honey bent over moving boxes made Bama drop his end of the bak.

"C'mon bruh what you doing" Ked asked as he followed Bama eyes. Dragging the bale closer to the wall, then sat it up against it. "Damn by cuz you can't be having all that ass out like that some folks can't handle it" Ked stated in a laughing matter. Quickly finishing unloading the other their bales, Laleel and Tom went back to the Audi while Ked talked to Honey and Bama hopped on the phone.

"Aye I was telling Sticky that we didn't find Auntie but we came across all of this"

"Well that's' cool cause I think she might have found something to fix all of this."

"Ok well be cool and I'm here if you need me, but for now I have to duck all of this weed off"

"Ok I'm about to call Sticky and let her know you just left."

Ked gave Honey a hug before he jumped inside of the truck. As he entered the Denali, Bama informed he that Gino and Rojas wanted a half of bale each. Grinning from the sound of money Ked shut the door and drove off, Migo Tom and Laleel was right behind them. As Honey let down the garage door she quickly called Sticky.

"Hello"

"What do you want me to do with all this weed?"

"What!? Honey what are you talking about now?"

"Ked just dropped it off and said that was for looking out"

"Ok but did he say anything about moma"

"Oh yeah, he dropped off her bag and it had a few of her things in it"

"That was it"

"Yeah that was it, he said that you knew everything else"

"Ok well lock up the house, because I need you to make another run"

"Girl it is to later to be making drops."

"Look this the last one I need you to go to Thomas Ville and drop a bag off to Redman"

"Hold on wait a minute, you talking about A.D right?"

"Yeah! He needs a bag, he hit me up"

"Girl I'm not going over that crazy boy house this late, he will have to wait"

"Alight let me finish what I'm doing I'll call you later."

Hanging up from talking to Sticky thinking about how she wanted her to go over that boy house this late. Know that he always be trying to hit on her. slightly smiling at the fact that it do be knida cute, how he be trying to run his game by making her laugh. Honey sat on the sofa going through her instagram page on her phone trying to see who was up.

T.H.N: Neko

"Tuck what it do?"

"Shiid bruh same ol same ol trying to get this money"

"Yeah, I'm still trying to bounce back from my hit"

"Yeah I heard about that, did you find out anything yet on who did it"

"Man it's so many haters out here but I think I got my man thou"

"Oh yeah who you think done that shit"

"You did old bitch ass nigga" Neko yelled out as he swung at Tuck."

Going back and forth sharing blows with each other until Tuck slipped and let Neko grab him. Taking him for a ride, lifting him up in the air just to bring him back down. Slamming him hard as ever on his back Then wrapped his arm around his neck and begun chocking him out. Realizing that ….had stop moving. Neko let him let him go and stood up. As people walked and drove by Neko gave him a few kicks and told him that's for snitching and setting me up. Everyday turned their heads and kept it moving.

Picking him up to lean him against his car, then laid him on the back seat. Making haste to get into the car, he notice Tuck begin to move. Hopping in and hauling ass around the corner to his home boy house. Blowing the horn as he pulled inside the driveway and cut across the grass to get closer to the front door. As his homeboy stepped on to the front porch, Neko climbed out the car. "Aye Trap help me get this nigga out the car." "Who dat cuz?"

"This punk ass nigga Tuck"

"Oh Hell yeah coz you finally caught up with that nigga."

Santching Tim out of the car and toting him inside the house. After securing him to an old wheel chair that was in the closet, Neko dashed him with a cup of cold water. Walking up in shock, Trap slapped him just to get his blood flowing.

"Now you gone tell me who was the little bitch from the city that you had Rob me."

"Bruh I don't know what you talking about,"

"Bitch you gone kiss my ass with yo momma lips if you ain't gone tell me who the fuck Robbed me."

"Bruh what's on Big B and tall P's I don't know what you talking about."

Nigga I put shit on crip and my momma all the time, I don't want to hear that shit. Trap get that nigga phone."

Hitting him in the knees with a hammer each time he felt like he was lying about which number was the right one. The sound of his knee caps crushing and the pain he was feeling made him sing like a mocking bird. As he collected everything that he needed from him, he reminded Tuck who he was. "Bitch you really thought something was going to happen to me down here in Bloomfield and I didn't get to the bottom of it. Come on cuz lets get rid of this nigga."

Chapter 8

T.H.N: Sticky

Rolling over in bed bumping into something Sticky quickly open her eyes. Forgetting that John-John had spent the night with her, she peeked under the covers to see if he had an early morning hard on. Seeing his swollen penis protruding in his boxers made her wet. Slowly making her way down to his boxers trying not to wake him up. Softly grasping his penis through his boxer hole as she positioned herself. Placing her mouth on his swollen man hood and begin going up and down while using her head to stroke him.

Feeling the warm and wet sensation of her mouth wrapped around him dick woke him up. Snatching the sheets off of them so he could see her at work. Looking at her looking up at him as she went up and down made him get even harder. Pulling Sticky up from giving him head to making her ride him. The more she bounced up and down on the dick, John-John started to forgive her for their little beef. As Sticky turned around on the dick, rolling her hips and bouncing her ass in his face.

John-John gripped and smacked her on the ass, biting on his bottom lip enjoying every minute of it. Letting her turn back around to face him before he slide to the edge of the bed. Holding on to Sticky as he got off the bed, stroking her as he stood there. Then begin to slowly turn around to lay her back on the bed. Placing her on bed and arranging her leg for them to be beside her head, as he drove shaft deep down inside of her fast and hard. Leaning in as he slowed down to kiss her on the lip and worked his way to her neck Caressing her body while slowly stroking her insides.

John-john stopped and stood up to scoot Sticky to the edge bed. Closing her legs to position her so that ass would hang off the bed just a little. Smacking her on the ass while Rubbing his dick up against her wet pussy. Sliding back inside of her making moan softly. Stroking her softly as he stared into her eyes. Feeling himself about to climax, he pulled out and got on his knees. Spreading her legs kissing on her inner thigh, working his way down to her kitty.

Licking and Sucking on her clit while figuring her. Sticky grabbed his head as she begin to climax for the fourth time. Hearing her moan as she rubbed on his head, he begun sticking his tongue inside of her. As she continued to cum, John-John stood up and flipped her over. Tooting her ass up in the air as he stuffed a pillow under her to keep it form go down to far. Pulling her closer to him as he placed himself inside of her slowly stroking her to find his grove as he looked at her ass bouncing up against him.

As found his grove he begin going faster. Sticky let out sexy moans missed with short screams as he continued to pound her from the back. "Get this pussy daddy" Sticky screamed as she threw it back at him. Smacking and rubbing her on the ass before he slid thumb in her asshole. Moving his thumb up and down while he slowly and softly stroked her insides. Changing the whole mood, sticky gripped the sheets as she put her head in a pillow. Slowly sliding forward each time he thrust himself inside of her. Feeling herself about to climax again, she bite the pillow and gripped the sheets even tighter.

Feeling a strong gush of wetness pushing on the head of his penis, he pulled out to watch her squirt. Watching her squirt everywhere greeted him up, he lifted her ass up in the air and started licking and sucking on her asshole. Sticking his tongue inside of her ass then pulled it out and brushed it up against it going up and down. Taking two figures and inserting them inside of her. Bending the slightly to press down on her G-spot while he rubbed back and forth on it. Making her climax again instantly.

John-John flipped her over and went right inside her. Penning her to the bed as he pound her fast and hard. Watching eyes roll in the back of her head made him smile. Reaching his climax at the same time Sticky did made it like ecstasy. An essential feeling made him lay on top of her and begun kissing her, sucking on her bottom lip then gave her another little smooch. Rolling over to the side of the bed, lying flat on his back while Sticky laid her head on his chest.

"John-John I just wanted to tell you thank you and I'm sorry?"

"Well I'm thanking you for helping me last night and I'm sorry for leaving you while you was locked up."

"It's no issue about last night me and my niggas like to get our hands dirty sometime. But about you leaving me that was fucked up."

"Man don't say that because it wasn't all my full way I left you. My momma made me do it because she said that my head wasn't where it needed to be."

"I told you I was coming home they didn't have nothing on me."

"I know but when they offered your life she and I both thought it was over with."

"Shied it's cool now cause I'm out and I'm up, but one thing don't ever go backwards."

"What's you talking about?"

"Man you left me and got with that lame ass nigga."

"Who you talking about? I ain't been with nobody but.... oh boy that was a onetime thing."

"Yeah whatever but you heard what I said. So what's up you gone cook breakfast"

"Boy stop I'm too tired to do anything right now." Sticky replied as she grabbed the remote control to turn on the T.V.

Flipping through channels seeing nothing but the breaking news sign in the top or bottom of the T.V Screen. Pausing for a minute to see what was being said and why it was on every channel down near.

News Reporter: The police are still looking for suspect, they say it was over a thousand rounds fired. And they are saying the key suspect to this murder and shooting is the owner of this vehicle. A 2008 Mercedes with the license plate that read HELL Raiser. This just in! They are saying the car belongs to an Eddie Ward and was reported stolen.

Just two days ago. Well that's all we have for now on this topic, Richard so we handing it over to you. But we will keep you posted." "Ok Tacy thank you for the exclusive update. Now other news Trump....

Before the reporter could finish Talking about Trump, Sticky had done changed the channel. "Come on Shawty lets clean up and go get something to eat." John-John said as he sat up in the bed. Jumping out the bed acting silly. Dancing around, as she made her way to John-John and started grinding on him.

"Oh yo ass can do all this dancing and shit but you can't cook a nigga nothing to eat."

"Ok, Ok I just didn't feel like cooking but what you want."

"Now we gone go out to eat now because I need you to drop me off at the spot."

"So you just gone dick me down like that and leave."

"Man don't start that mess we both got shit to do."

"Yea nigga whatever I'll let you slide with that one because I do got a lot going on"

As they walked inside of the bathroom, Sticky looked back at John-John to see if he was watching her ass like always. Turning back around smiling and laughing as she thought to herself he is still the same. Turning on the water letting it warm up as she grabbed her wash rag then wet it. Cleaning herself up then Reached over and did the same to him. Liking the way she softly held his dick in her hand as she washed it off, he began to harden back up. Lifting Sticky up and placing her on the counter. Then graded her legs as he went down on her.

Kissing and nibbling on her pussy lips, while he jerked himself off to get fully erected. As he continued sucking on her clit, he felt the swollenness of his penis and knew he was ready. Standing up and slowly working his way inside of her, while he pulled her to him. Putting one hand behind her neck and the other on her ass, as he gently stroked her. Kissing her neck as she let out soft moans and wrapped arms around his neck. Beginning to go faster and harder, Sticky tighten her grip. Going from soft sexy monas to biting her lip and Screaming out I'm Cumming, John-John speeded up. Removing his hand form around her neck to place it on here other ass cheek. Squeezing her ass and pulling her close while taking quick and fast pumps. Tightening his cheeks together as he climaxed and slowed down his strokes.

Laying his head up against Sticky to give her a peck on the forehead, before he looked back at Sticky and gave her a little grin to acknowledge that he did his tang. Still sitting on the bathroom counter smiling watching him walk away while biting on her bottom lip. Knowing that he still had the key to her heart. Jumping off the counter to stick the rag back under the warm water. While cleaning herself up she began to think about the statement Zoe was about to make, before they aired the park out.

Rushing out of the bathroom to get dressed, she grabbed her phone off the dresser and called Nino.

"Hello"

"I hope you are woke, cause I need you to fire up the torch"

"Now you talking my language, so what time does this party start"

"Give me about 15 – 20 minutes and I'll be over."

"Ok I'll have everything prepped and ready to go."

Seeing that look in Sticky's eyes John-John knew she was up to something. As soon as she hung up the phone he approached her to see what she was planning.

"Are what's up? What are you about to do?"

"What are you talking about?"

"Come on Shawty I know that look, I done seen it many of times before."

"Oh nothing just thinking about old boy from last night."

"Yeah I knew it was something so what you gone do?"

"Oh I'm about to drop you off and I'm going to handle business."

Opening up the bedroom door to see Honey leant up against her room door, with rollers in her hair and a bath robe with matching house shoes. Unfolding her arms and smacking her teeth as Sticky and John-John made their way down the hall way.

"So you get to lay up and get your rocks off but I can't get me non"

"Girl whatever, that's all you do is lay on your back. You ain't helped not once since momma been gone."

"That's what the police get paid for I'm not about to be out there getting in trouble, I love my momma an all but I can't go to jail."

"Whatever Girl I'll keep you posted I guess."

"Yeah you do that and John-John don't think you can just come back in here slanging dick when you want too."

"Alight little big sis, oh yea my boy Kebo said get at him."

"Didn't he sign to G-Unit South or was that Brick Squad"

"Man look I ain't about to get into all of that just hit him up, the number is"

Calling out the number as they exited the house. Seeing the glow in her face, he just shook his head as he got inside the car. As they pulled the driveway a text came through his phone that read "Are we still on for the night." Texting back yea" then put the phone back in his pocket as he sat back in the seat.

T.H.N: Eddie Haitian

"Damn these fucking Asian are swift and smart as he'll" Eddie thought to himself as he did surveillance. Watching them off load trucks and take selected boxes to one shop, conformed everything that Queen told him. Taking a few pictures of the back end of the plaza before leaving. Making his way across the highway form a Lawrenceville subdivide, to pull up in the front of the plaza. Finding a descry parking spot to resume his Surveillance. With not to much activity going on in the front, Eddie get out of the car and went inside of Pho Dai Luy. Taking a look around as he walked to the counter to place his order.

"How may I help you" the old lady asked in a strong Asian accent

"Umm… let me get some shrimp fried Rice and some braised wings."

"Would you like anything to drink or would that be all sir?"

"Yeah let me get a larger sprite"

"Ok that will be $8.20"

As he paid the small Asian lady, he notice a group of Asian coming form the back in suits and ties. Taking a sit to wait on his order, he pulled out his phone and started recording footage of the restaurant. Trying to play it off by acting as if he was going live on Facebook. Walking around in the buffet to see if its any weak spots or exits that he could come through quick and unseen. Hearing the old lady call for him to pick up his order, Eddie turned his recorder off and placed his phone it in his back pocket. While picking up his order another group of Asian came from the back, but only this time they was dressed in jeans and white T's with blue bandana hanging out of their back pocket.

All of them was carrying black duffle bags. Walking behind them as they left the restaurant, one of the Asian stopped and step to the side. Giving him a crazy stare as he let him walk by. Eddie nodded his head in acknowledgment as he walked pass them and went to his car. Sitting the food on the Roof of the car, while acting as if he lost keys just to see what type of car they climbed into. Once they had pulled out of their parking spot, Eddie quickly jumped inside of his car and pulled out behind them.

Trying his best to go unnoticed as they moved through traffic.

T.H.N: Nino

"Yeah little nigga you better talk up today" Nino stated as he lifted the torch to make sure it was working right. Then went to fill his favorite two buckets halfway with water and the rest with ice. Sitting the buckets a few feet in front of Zoe and then asked him if he knew what they was for. Laughing at him as he tried to jump around in the seat to break free. Slapping him across the head making him sit still, before he walked out the shed and into the house.

Unlocking the front door to let Sticking in. "What's up bruh where there nigga at?" Sticky asked as she walked inside of the house popping her Knuckles. Smiling as he pointed to the back, Nino liked to see her that way. Shutting the door and followed right behind her. As they entered the shed Sticky wasted no time, walking over to Zoe and snatched him up by the shirt. Punching him two or three time before asking him about her mother again. Knowing that he had the where about of her Sticky let it be known that she wasn't going to play with him.

"My nigga who got my momma?"

"You should have killed me when you had a change."

"So now you want to play tough, when I know you are a little bitch.

"Untie me and I'll show you who the bitch is."

Getting madder by the minute as she went back and forth with him. Nino turned on the torch and gentle moved Sticky to the side. Grasping Zoe by the neck pulling him in closet to him, as he whispered in his ear.

"Stop playing with me" then burned his chest with the fire. Letting his chest and shirt burn for a few minutes, before reaching into the bucket and grabbed the small cup filled with water to put him out.

"Now are you going to keep playing or are you going to talk"

"Fuck you pussy its mud life I ain't got shit to say."

Claiming, he was just acting if he was Haitian the other night. "Coming on bruh you don't know what you want to be, Haitian or from New Orleans" Sticky stated as she walked a little bit closer Nino stopped her before she could get any closer and told her to let him handle it. Giving him the look as if she was dying for some of the action, he just signed his hands in a motion telling her to chill.

Walking off to let him have that little bit. As she decided to have a little fun of her own. Waiting for Nino to take his focus off of her. As soon as she saw him burning Zoe again she want to beating up his moma. Nino sat the torch down and ran to pull Sticky off of her. "Look I got him talking so just give me a few minutes before you attack again. Hell I already ain't been feeding them, that's punishment enough." Nino said as he walked back over to Zoe. Picking up two silver spoons and held them in front of the torch."

Letting them get reddish orange before sitting the torch down. Placing both spoons over Zoe's eyes melting them close. Smelling cooked flesh made Sticky gag just a little. Shaking the smell and holding her composure, she came up with a bright idea. Running it by Nino before she took off with it. Sending the discomfort look on his face she knew that he wasn't feeling it, but he still gave her the go ahead to handle her business. Taking a rubber mallet and begin beating Peaches and the little girl.

"While Nino continued Working on Zoe, she beat and bruise them. Making sure they took an ass whipping from hell before cutting them loose from the chair. Tying them back together with some more Zippy ties. Nino took a quick break to help Sticky put them in the back of Zoe's car. On the way back through the house, Nino stopped Sticky to tell her everything that Zoe told him. "Man the kid say, he was just trying to impress his step father so he could get some work from him.

"So did he say who was his step daddy was and why they picked my mom to rob and kidnap?

"Yeah that's the crazy part. His step dad used to date your mom."

"Oh shit! That's where I remember that name Eddie warred from."

"So you do know him?"

"Yeah and it was on the new this morning that his car was stolen, but it was all part of the cap."

"Ok well check this they got a restaurant down town that got a hidden Room where they do their dirt in."

"Ok well what I'm about to do well bring him out of hiding out or make the cops do their job."

"You sure you want the cops in this."

"Shied it's too late they been in it form the jump, so now they just gone have to work for real."

"Well let me go put up everything and we will see how this play out."

While waiting for Nino to come back there was a knock at the front door. "Oh shit" Sticky said to herself as she waked back to the front door to peep out the peep hole. Seeing that it was Q made her feel move relaxed, but she knew that was a sign to go ahead and make her move. Opening the door grabbing Q by the hand and pulled him with her.

"While hey to you too." Q said as he followed behind her

"No time to talk, I need you to drive."

Hopping behind the wheel as sticky got in the back with Peaches and the kid. Telling him where to go and what to do when they got there. 30 minutes later they was arriving at Southern Regional Hospital. Sticky lean over and open the door and pushed them out of the car as it slowly turned around at the entrance. Pulling out into traffic headed back to Nino's house, Sticky filled Q in on what's was going on.

Chapter 9

T.H.N: Honey

Later that even while snooping around Queen's house, Honey found a black galaxy 6 on the floor behind the head board. As she took the phone off the charger and turned it on, a brown skinned guy with dreads appeared on the screen with a white chick. Scratching her head out of confusion, Not knowing who he was and why his phone was at her mom's house. She quickly took her phone out of the back pocket and call sticky. "Come on Sticky pick up the phone" Honey mumbled to herself.

"Hello"

"Hey Girl I found this phone in momma room do you know who it belong to?"

"Umm what do it look like?"

"It's a black galaxy 6….. Oh my God who was that in the back ground."

"Oh that was nothing we just handle a lil business that's all but what do the phone say when you turn it on."

"It say 360° player with a picture of a dude with some dreads and a white girl."

"A nigga with dread…. Umm it might be this guy that lost his phone that night momma got missing. He showed up looking for it the next day."

"Oh so od you know how to get in touch with him."

"Yeah I got some number he gave me in my phone, give me a see."

Looking through her phone to find his contact information, Zoe continue to let out loud strange noises. Hearing pounding mixed with screams of pain, Honey eyes got bigger and bigger each time she heard one of them strange noises. Pressing the phone up against her ear trying to hear every little noise that came through the speaker. She felt as if she was watching an action movie but could only hear it. Jumping from being started by Sticky voice as she came back on the phone. Honey let out a little giggle has she asked for the info.

"What's the number?"

"470 – 343 – 7383"

"Damn that's a lot of threes in that number but who do I ask for?"

"You would pay attention to something like that but the guy name is Boobie." Did you say Bobbie, like in Totties Boobies"

"Girl I don't know the nigga just told me his name was Boobie"

"Ok I'll call him and tell him that I found his phone."

"Ok and be careful because I still don't know if he was in on it or not."

"I will and Sticky I still want to know what you are doing?.... Hello! Hello!"

Getting hung up on made Honey feel some type of way. She began talking shit to herself as she dialed up Boobie's number. "This bitch thinks she's the female John. Gotti or somebody hanging up on me like that. Hell I'm the big sister around this bitch, I'm gone put her in her place when she got....Oh hello"

"I don't know who you talking about but they done pissed you off."

"Oh my God you heard me, I'm so sorry. Is this boobie?"

"Yeah this me who is this."

"I found your phone at my mom's house and my sister gave me your number."

"Ok that's what's up, I will be over to get it in about 30 minutes to an hour."

"Um well actually I'm about to hit Southlake Mall so you can meet me there."

"That's even better for me because I'm coming out of Griffin"

"Ok well just call me when you get there and I'll meet you in the food court"

"Ok say no mo"

As they hung up the phone, Honey went inside of Queen's night stand and pulled out her Taser. Placing it inside of her small Fendi hand purse before leaving the room. Getting slightly emotional from being at Queen's house and she's not there to run her out of her room. Wiping her face from the few tears that fell from her eye as she walking out the house.

T.H.N: Queen

"Nigga where the fuck you been? You could have at least fed a bitch"

"Shut you boma cloth yapping, I brought you some Chinese food."

"Oh you been spying on them damn Asians, haven't you?"

"Why? What's it to you."

"I'm just saying, I can get you in the door with them or you can do it your way."

"Yeah right, I rather do it my way them to let you fuck over me again."

"Ok well just let me go you have everything you need now"

"No! No! No! You don't get away that easy, you still got to pay."

"Well damn gone kill me because I don't want to be sitting around like this, All tied up and shit. You already then fucked up my face."

"You keep running them dick beater, I'm gone, beat you some more."

Queen got quiet, then asked Eddie if he could at least undo one of her hands so they could eat. Looking at her with a look that would kill, if looks could kill before making his way over to her. Cutting her loose while standing over her looking at her breast. Biting then licking his lips remembering how she used to shake her breast in face and make him suck them. Glancing up at him catching the lust in his eyes, set off an idea inside Queen mind.

As soon as her hand was free, she took it and Rubbed it down Eddie's chest then gripped his dick. "I knew little Eddie still wanted this pussy or do you call him something else now" Queen giggled while removing her hand from his swollen penis, and started eating. Hating that he really never shook his feelings for Queen and knew that she knew it too. Eddie sat down at the small table that was in the room and began looking at his footage. The more he reviewed the query thing, the more he realized that it wasn't enough.

Sliding back from the table to paste the floor. Verbally going over everything to Queen just to see if she had a few pointers. She was always better and spotting things that he couldn't see. Going back and forth straightening with Queen. While helping Eddie with his plan, she was still working on her own to scape. Waiting for the right time to make her move, she continued to throw subjections out.

Eddie passed back and forth listening to Queen, the more she talked the more he started to get side track. He walked over to her, unzipped his pants pulling out his man hood, and told her to suck it like she used to. Grabbing his dick with her free hand and placing it in her mouth. Jerking it back and forward while bobbing her head on it. Thinking to herself it's about time, Knowing that Eddie was a sucker for head, it wouldn't be long before he wanted to fuck. Removing her hand from his manhood to grab Eddie's hand. Guiding his hand down her body to place it gently on her warm and wet kitty.

Beginning to Rub his hand gently on her warm and wet kitty.

Beginning to Rub his head in a circular motion as he eased one finger inside of her. Feeling Queen's wet Kitty made all of Eddie's blood Rush to his manhood, Making him swell up even more. Popping his dick out of her mouth so he could lean over to grab the pair of scissors. Cutting her other hand free, then pushed her back onto the bed. Lifting her legs up and dragging her closer to him as he inserted himself inside of her. stroking her softly as he found her spot.

After an hour and fifteen of unwanted sex Queen was finally able to make her move. With Eddie laying in the bed sound asleep. Queen slid out of the bed and grabbed her Robe. Quickly putting it on and tied it tight as she made her way to the door. Quietly opening the hotel Room door, slipping out trying her best not to make no noise. As she pulled the door up she noticed Eddie feeling around in the bed looking for her. Seeing him opening his eyes and looked dead at the door, Locking eyes before she shut the door. Queen turned around and took off Running.

Eddie slung the door open, fumbling as he stood there necked with one leg in his gym shorts. Trying his best to keep an eye on Queen as he put his shorts on. Running to the car and jumping behind the wheel, wasting no time pulling out the parking spot. In and out of the lite traffic trying his hardest to get close enough so he could catch her. Seeing her turning down a side street, Eddie switched lanes and drove on to the curb. Hitting Queen with the car making her fly onto the hood.

Quickly slapping the car into reverse making Queen Roll of the hood. Then shifted back into drive and ran Queen over. As he continued going up the small hill next to the Town's Inn on Tara blood headed into Riverdale, he saw cars pulling up left and right to check on Queen. Getting far away from the scene as possible, as he began talking to himself. Hoping and wishing nobody wrote down his tag or took any pictures. Meanwhile Queen laid there unresponsive, as the crowd stood there talking about what happened.

15 minutes later the abundance arrived and slowly placed Queen inside, while the police continued questioning the crowd. But no one could give any concrete statements of what happened. They all just know that it was a black or dark colored car that they see going over the hill. Taking Queen to the nearest hospital to run tests to identify her. Being naked and just barely covered by her robe was no help to the cops.

Laying there connected to the EKG machine as the doctors in and out the room. Queen was finally diagnosed to be in a lite Coma and it was not yet confirmed who she was.

Chapter 10

T.H.N: Sticky

Two days later Sticky was awakened to some bad news. Receiving a call from Nino to inform her that Zoe had escaped. Sitting up on the edge of the bed with the phone up to her ear.

"I searched every yard by the house."

"Damn, how did this happen again?"

"She'd little sis I got up to check my house and went out back to make sure everything was locked up and that nigga was gone."

"How the fuck he get lose and he can't see Right?"

"Well shid he must can see cause ain't no way that he could get away like that and as far as how he got loose, he use the torch to burn the ropes."

"Ok well I'll have to put the word, but you know it's kill on sight now."

"Hell you should have been let me kill that nigga"

"Yeah I know but I needed that info out of him."

"Well next time you bring someone to me, ain't no letting them go."

"Say no mo, but let me get up so I can put my ears to the street and see what's new."

Hanging up the phone then place her hands on her head, Feeling like things couldn't get any worse. Sticky got up and got herself together, thinking about all of the possibilities he could be. Walking out the room and to the kitchen she notices Honey laying on the couch. The closer she got the better she could hear. Honey was laying on the couch having phone sex with lord who knows. Sticky shook her head and entered the kitchen, opening the freezer door and pulled out 2 breakfast hot pockets then threw them in the microwave.

Shutting the door to the microwave made Honey jump. Sticky giggled to herself as she open the refrigerator to grab the … off the top rack. As she leaned back up Honey was standing there with her hand on the wall and one on her hip.

"Uh umm girl you need to wash them hand better you be putting them everywhere"

"Whatever girl my pussy clean and what are you doing up?" I thought you was going to sleep in

"Yeah I was but I got a call that make me get up"

"Oh so how is everything coming along"

"I'm getting closer but my prime lead just got away."

"Oh my God girl you are starting to sound like the police."

"Bitch don't play with me!"

"I'm just saying, but anyway I got this little event that I'm going to tonight you should come. There's going to be all kinds of ballers there."

"Nah I'm good but you can keep you ear to the streets to see if one of them knows something."

"Girl ain't nobody thinking about our momma but yo….I meant us."

"Yeah I know you ain't worried about her but all them little drug dealer you fuck with shopped with Queen so they might know something.

Sticky grabbed her hot pockets out of the microwave and the Oj off the counter. Bumping into Honey with her shoulder as she walked pass. As she headed back to her room Honey came up behind her. Snatching her backwards by her shirt while delivering a blow to the side of her face. Sticky dropped her food on the floor and turned around and rushed Honey. "I'm sick of your smart ass mouth." Honey yelled out as she continued to punch Sticky. Tripping over the sofa as they went blow for blow with each other.

Rolling off the couch onto the floor tussling to see who was going to get on top. Sticky muscled her way on top of Honey and pent her arms down with her knees. Hitting her multiple times in the face, before Honey flipped her off of her by lifting up her hips and turning on her side. They both jumped up and squared off, talking shit to one another as they stood there. Sticky inched up slowly just enough to hit Honey in the mouth.

"Oh shit, bitch you done did it now."

"Come on bitch you done lost it, all you want to do is lay up."

"I'm gone show you who gone be laying up somewhere."

Honey stopped in to swing at Sticky and she took off running. Honey shot behind her, chasing her around the living Room. Quickly cutting through the living room and jumping over the sofa, Sticky turned around and stuck her tongue out at Honey. Going from side to side as Honey still tried to catch her, Sticky grabbed a pillow and tossed at Honey and told her just to give up. Getting frustrated with Sticky because she was on the other end of the sofa laughing. Knowing that she would never catch her she just sat down, and waved her hand at her telling her to gone about her business.

Sticky hurried and ran behind the love seat to make sure Honey didn't try no funny business. As she got behind the love seat she looked over to Honey and noticed she was crying. In scantly changing from play mood to being concerned, she asked Honey what was wrong.

"Playing around with you made me miss momma even more."

"Yeah I know right I miss her too."

"I was just thinking how she would come in and whip us both for fighting and running around the house."

"That's why I'm fighting so hard to find her."

"Did you check out that restaurant that Teezy was talking about?"

"What restaurant?"

"The Jamaican restaurant downtown, you know the one we use to go to"

"Oh shit that's right, I was supposed to go down there"

"Yeah because he might be the key to it all"

"Do you know who Eddie Word is?"

"Duh! That's mom's ex-boyfriend"

Coming from behind the love seat to have a seat, Sticky sat there in confusion. Trying to figure out why he would be after Queen.

Sticky knew it was only one way to find out. She hopped out of the love seat and headed for the door. As she opened the front door she looked back at Honey and told her to come on.

"Girl you know I'm too pretty for all this gangsta shit."

"Girl come on here, we are just about to spend some time together."

"Oh so you want to spend some time with me now? Huh?"

"Child hush just, come on"

Sticky stood there wasting for Honey to walk out the door. And as she passed by Sticky she giggled don't make me give you around two. Sticky laughed as she shut the door behind her.

T.H.N: Eddie

"Who dis?"

"Eddie it's me Zoe."

"Rude boy! Where the fuck you been?"

"Look I'll tell you everything but I need you to come pick me up."

"Ok but where are you?"

"I don't know I'll have to get someone to tell you."

Handing the phone back to an old lady and man to give Eddie there location. As he sat there waiting for them to get off the phone, he heard the person telling Eddie how he was wrong having him out there by himself. The longer they stayed on the phone the more she explained Zoe's condition and wondered what happen to him. Eddie quickly got off the phone, so he wouldn't have to keep lying to the old woman.

As they sat inside of the Waffle parking lot off of boat rock Rd and camp creek. The man went back inside to grab Zoe a bit to eat. Meanwhile Zoe sat there with the old lady on the side of the building. As she waiting with him she asked more questions and told Zoe, if he was in a bad environment and needed a way out that he could come stay with them. Before he could answer her he heard a horn repeatedly honking. Taking his attention off of the old lady to try to focus on the car ahead of him. Looking through the small hole in his eye lid form where it didn't connect when they melted his eyes shut.

Zoe stood up as Eddie came flying up the street. He couldn't tell for sure if that was him, but he just had a good feeling. Eddie jumped out the car and ran over to Zoe. Checking him out, seeing how bad he was fucked over. Eddie reached into pocket and pulled out a knot of money. Rolling off a few hundred then handed them to the lady for staying with Zoe until he got there. While he help Zoe inside the car, the old man came walking around the corner with the food.

As Eddie got behind the wheel, the old man stuck the food inside the window and sat in Zoe's lap. Eddie shut his door and started up the car. Backing out of the parking lot, trying not to let the old couple see his license tay. Not trusting no one but his day one niggas. And soon as that thought came across his mind his phone rang. "Hello."

"Yo Rude boy! You had two chicks come by here about 30 minutes ago"

"Did they say what they wanted or who they was?"

"Nah! They just wanted to know if you still worked at the restaurant."

"Ok say no more and I'm still working on that lick with the Asians."

"Keep your head and keep me posted, if you need us you know where we at?"

As soon as he hung up the phone he turned to Zoe and to him to enlighten him on everything he knew. Eddie sat back in the driver seat and gripped the wheel with one hand as he listened to Zoe.

Chapter 11

T.H.N: Fox's News

"Well it has been A month and a half since we heard anything about these two cases. The case of hit and run on Eve Mae Arm wood and the case of assault and battery on Peaches Adam. They are saying that the both are tied to each other in some way. And the key to all of this is Mr. Ward. But the police stated that he hasn't been seen. And he has a warrant out for his arrest for questioning.

Doctors are saying that Ms. Arm wood is suffering from a light coma but is coming around. And Ms. Adam will go under leg surgery with in a day or soon. They have tightened up the security here at Southern Regional Hospital. If anyone has any information please contact our crime hotline: 1-800-45 Crime. Well that's all I have for now Sam, but if anything new accrue I will be sure to keep you posted.

Thank you Tay; Precedent Trump is saying that he didn't know anything about the meeting between his son and the Russian....

T.H.N: Sticky

Turning the T.V off as her and Honey jumped off the sofa in excitement. Hugging each other as they danced around in a circle.

"Coming on we got to go see momma."

"Sticky I'm about to cry I'm so happy they found her."

"Me to so let's go."

Quickly picking up the plastic Glock 9 and her keys from the coffee table and headed for the door. Honey came Right behind her putting on some peaches and cream lip gloss.

T.H.N: Eddie

"Damn that Bitch just don't want to die."

"What's that Pop's?"

"That bomba clot Queen, she's a pain in the ass. I don't need her alive."

"So what we gone do?"

"We got to finish the job, I have to send Chop to handle her. We have to get at these Asians."

"I feel you pops but it ain't much that I can do now with my eyes melted shut."

"We gone use that to our advantage don't worry."

Taking the phone out of his joggers he quickly dialed chop's number. As soon as possible he answered the call, Eddie told him to meet him at the spot pronto. Before he could reply Eddie had done hung up the phone. Confiscating his keys off of the counter then coming back to guide Zoe out of the house.

T.H.N: Queen

"Did you have to get so many balloons?"

"Yeap I sure did I want my Momma to know she's been missed"

"Well hell at least get them out of my face."

Moving the balloons out of her was as she opened the door to Queen's Room. As she walked into the Room she heard a toilet flush and a door begin to open. Sitting the flowers down on the

Roller away tray holder, while signaling Honey to be quiet. As the door continued to open Sticky reached for her pistol. Patting her hip for getting that she left it inside of the car she begun scanning the room for something hard and heaving. A middle age man came out of the bathroom.

"What are you doing here!?" Sticky asked.

"Yeah Boobie what are you doing here?" Honey requisitioned

"I just came to check on her when I found out where she was."

"Well how have you been here?"

"I been here for about 20 to 30 minutes."

"And they just let you in here like that"

"Yeah I told them I was her old man because I really wanted to see her."

"Look my nigga I don't know what you got going on but I need for you to leave."

"Man Shawty I'm on yo side, Honey telling her what I told you."

"Yeah Sticky he don't mean no harm, he told me all about the crush he got on

"You know that shit don't mean nothing to me this my momma we talking about I'm gone chill because it's about her right now. But anything crazy that's yo ass."

"Well Damn ain't you blunt, but it's under stood."

Honey took the balloon and tied them to a chair in the corner of the room, while Boobie and Sticky stood around the bed. Grasping Queen by the hand while she laid there unconscious. Sticky begin to cry as she talked to Queen, hoping that the sound of her voice would bring around. Honey wrapped her arms around Sticky, trying her best not to cry.

"Umm well look I'm going to step outside and let you girls have a minute alone"

"Ok" Honey replied

As Boobie stepped outside the room, Sticky and Honey stood there in grief. Letting tears Roll their faces. Ten minutes done passed and their alone time was interrupted. A nurse walked into the room on begin checking her IV and the EKG Machine, to make sure she was okay. While standing there sticky felt her phone vibrating in her back pocket. Pulling out the phone to see who was calling. It was her little cousin Ked G. turning to Honey and showing her the phone to het her know, that she was about to take the call.

"What's up Cuz?"

"Shiid nothing Foolie, I just wanted to tell you that I see were Auntie was"

"Yeah I seen it too, me and Honey are up here now."

"Ok that's what's up I'll swing by later."

"That's cool, you know she needs all the love she can get right now."

"Yea I know, but aye check this out."

"What's up?"

"Aye look we are on big time, I just met a new pug but it's something fishie about him."

"What do you mean?"

"I don't think we could trust but we could work him them turn around and get them."

"Shiid Keep going because I know its move to it."

While leaning against the hallway window listening to Ked, Boobie came walking back down the hallway. The closer he got the better the tray of food smelt. Boobie opened the tray filled with fried chicken and a side of Mac and cheese.

"You want some?"

"Now I'm good but Honey might, she's in the Room still"

"Come on Shawty don't act like that I got enough for all of us."

"You just gone make a bitch eat some chicken, you lucky I'm a little hungry."

Boobie laughed as she took a piece of chicken off of the fray and went back to talking on the phone. The more information that she received the more she wanted in.

"Aye Cuz hold on for one minute."

"Ok"

"Hello"

"Say sticky what we doing tonight."

"Well I'm at the hospital Right now John-John"

"Ok shied just hit when you get time."

"Ok I will baby" Sticky stated right before hang up the phone with him.

"Ked you still there."

"Yea I'm here."

"Ok finish telling me about this nigga Cranberry"

Walking towards the Room to throw away her chicken bone a dark brown heavy set dude approached the Room as well.

"Umm excuse me can I help you."

"Now I'm good I just came to see my auntie."

"Uh who are you? Because I never seen you before."

"Never mind I'll just see her another time."

Turning around trying to walk away from the door. Sticky took two steps behind him and grabbed him by his arm. Jerking his arm away from her made him drop the syringe full of morphine. Sticky looked at him a "What the fuck look" and before she knew it she had dropped her phone and went to swing. Within two minutes of their tussle, Honey and Boobie stuck their head out of them. Honey shot pass Boobie and jumped on guy's back placing him in a choke hold.

Sticky came off the wall swinging as the guy tried his best to throw Honey off of his back. Finally tossing Honey off his back after receiving multiple blows to the face. Honey and Sticky both squared off with him waiting for him to make the first move. As he stood there with a bloody nose he knew he couldn't go back without handling what he came for. Looking at the syringe that rolled next to the wall, trying to see the best was to pick it back up.

As soon as he took open step forward they both took off on him. Backing back in to the corner trying to avoid as many hits as possible. Boobie finally sat the tray of chicken down and Ran over to help. Pulling up his pants from the lite sag then yelled out "I'm DJ Uncle Boobie bitch" and went head first. A nurse came walking around the corner and started screaming for help. Seeing them jumping on that guy made her panic.

As Clayton County police came flying around the corner yelling out freeze, they passed for a brief moment. Watching them get on his ass was like watching a movie. They quickly snapped out of it and ran over to help him. Making over one get on the floor, so they could put restrains on them. After they got everyone cuffed up, they sat them against the wall. Trying to figure out what happen while having a nurse check them out.

"Umm excuse me Miss, but I have talked everyone and everything is pointing at you."

"Yeah I know I hear what they said I'm right here with yall."

"Ok well could you tell me what happen?"

"Hell that fat mother fucker over there was talking about he was some kin to my momma. But when I asked him who he was he tried to walk off so I grabbed his arm to ask him something and he tried to hit me so we got to fighting. Oh yea he dropped that needle over there against the wall too."

"So you don't know him, is that what you telling me?"

"Yea that's what I'm saying I don't know him and he tried to kill my momma."

"Yo cuz you good" Ked yelled as him and Migo Tom waked down the hall. The closer they got the officer rushed over and told them not to come any closer. "Man I'm just trying to check on my family" Ked stated as he stood there grilling the officer. Turning around and waking away from Ked to go back other to crime scene.

"Alight this is how we gone handle this, we are going to let you all go with just a warning because we know that yall have been thru a lot with your mom. But we are going to lock this one up for attempted Murder." Officer Hill stated as he uncuffe everyone but Chop. Feeling a sense of relief

Sticky rubbed her wrist and took a deep breath. Picking up her phone as walked over to ked.

"What's up cuz? What made you come up here so soon?"

"Shiid I hear you hitting with somebody so I came"

"You miss yo big cuz in action."

"Yea we was giving it to that nigga, but I'm glad they ain't look us up. I'm to cute to go to jail." Honey added while reaching out for a hug.

While standing there catching up with ked as they waited for the police to care out, Boobie eased his way back into the room.

Feeling out of place by not knowing them, he felt better in the room with Queen.

"Aye cuz who that was"

"Who you talking about?" Sticky question

"That just went in the room with Auntie."

"Oh that's Boobie he's cool he just got thanks for momma."

"Tell that Big Head nigga he better start announcing himself"

"Hey where's that chocolate boy at that you had a few days ago." Honey asked

"Who you talking about Bama"

"Yeah that's him."

"Oh he's somewhere trying to get off some more of that gas."

"Speaking of good gas let's take a ride to finish our talk" Sticky implied

"Ok that sounds good to me but first let me handle something."

Herring to Queen's room and quickly coming back out, Honey spoke out "Damn that was fast". Ked just smiled at her as they walked off. Catching a nurse checking him out he quickly detoured and made his way over to her. "What's up I'm Ked G A.K.A the drip God" Ked stated as his opening line to get his Mac on. Standing there waiting for him to finish getting his Mac on Sticky replied to everything that they talked about earlier.

T.H.N: Eddie

"Zoe how bad is your seeing"

"Pop I can only see just a little out of the corner of my eyes."

"Ok that's good enough, I just need you to be able to shoot"

"You ain't afraid that I might hit you?"

"Not at all you will be in front of me and the Zoe pound will be backing us."

"Ok say no more."

As they sat in the car waiting for everyone else to pull up, Eddie checked their guns and finished telling Zoe the plan. Fifteen minutes later six cars and one RAM 1500 pulled up next to them. Eddie jumped out of the car and said "it's show time." Every car had three people inside. Everyone adjusted their attire while Eddie pulled the wheel chair out of his trunk. Helping Zoe into the chair then placed the Tommy Gun in his lap and covered it with a short and thick blanket.

Talking shit and cracking jokes with others as they walked inside of the restaurant. Seeing the same small Asians lady behind the county Eddie knew that it was going down as usual. She only worked on the day that the shipment came in. Giving Haitian Rob the look before asking to be scattered. The small Asian lady rang them up for the buffet and informed them to seat themselves. Within five to seven minutes after they sat down a group of black guys with blue bandannas sat down behind them.

While they enjoyed their meal waiting for the right time to make their move, Haitian Rod noticed that the big guy that looked like LeBron kept looking at the table. But before he could say a word Eddie had done tapped his foot under the table. Without saying a word he looked back at the entrance door. A small group of Asians came walking through the door. Some in business suites and others in white T's and Jeans. Waiting for them to walk to the back before they got out of their seat. Everybody quickly took their position, Rolling Zoe in front of the counter as they ducked taped and zippy tied the old lady.

Making it quick as they hit the kitchen entrance door. Every Asian that wasn't with the movement took off running screaming and speaking Chinese as they duck and hide behind kitchen appliances. Eddie signal direction for them to split up into a small group of two and spread out.

Laying down cover fire as everyone got up, and disbursed into three groups. Eddie heard gun fire coming from the restaurant.

T.H.N: Zoe

Hearing the bell on the entrance door got Zoe's attention. Looking very hard through the cracks in his eyelids, he noticed that it was back up for the Asians. Spraying any and everything that was in front of him.

T.H.N: Neko

"Trapp my boy, we are in a real live movie."

"Man cuz we need to get out of here it too much going."

"Hell now, you think I'm about to let this bitch pull this job off and we don't get nothing off it. This bitch got to pay" Neko said as he laid behind the flipped over dinner table. Thinking in his head that Trapp was right, but vengeance was too heavy on his heart.

Peeping from around the table every few seconds to see what was going on. He spotted an Asian rolling and crawling on the floor. And within a few seconds he was standing over the guy in the wheelchair. Placing a bullet right through his head.

"Damn Cuz I hope that nigga was talking about the same Queen we looking for"

"Oh so now you worried."

"Now cuz I'm just saying I hope it's the same bitch"

"What if it ain't we gone go down just for being here."

"Alight cuz just five more minutes they are heading to the back now."

T.H.N: Eddie

Finally making it to the back office getting their hands on the head Asian. Eddie and Haitian Rob demanded for every Asian to put their gun down. Having their boss at gun point they stood there waiting to get a clean shot without hitting the boss. Pressing against his head with the pistol while yelling "Put your guns down." Eddie knew they were outnumbered and he had to outsmart them. Trying to control them by controlling their boss. Eddie always used the "kill the head everything else will follow" Motto.

After five long minutes of having a standoff with them, they finally dropped their weapons. Eddie made the boss open up the safe, while Rob made another one take him to the stash spot. Keeping four of his guys with him to help confiscate all of the money out of the safe, while the other four went behind Rob. And within a second it was more gun fire taking place. More Asian had enter from the dinning. Eddie knew it had to be moved, once he heard the sound of the Tommy gun going off.

Hurrying to secure the bags before the Asians in the room got any bright ideas. Eddie made them crawl into a corner while they dragged the money by the office door. Keeping the boss right next to him for insurance as he backed out of the office. Bumping into Haitian Zac as he cashed out the room.

"Wait a minute Eddie it's too much heat faming form that way."

"Ok but where is Rob and them?"

"It's only Rob, Black and Ty"

"Damn we have took to many losses, on the count of three you shoot low and I go high"

"Ok on my count…1….2….3" Zac replied as he began counting.

As soon as he got to three they released gun fire. Running out of ammo and quickly releasing the clips to reload. A loud clinging sound came from the medal door as it flew open, and shots ranged out. Seeing the Asian drop to the floor made Eddie feel a lot better. Waiting to see who was behind them rescue, they emerged form behind the small wall.

Seeing the familiar face from the dinner area made Rob come out of hiding with his pistol drawn.

"That's how you going to act when I just saved your life."

"I don't trust no one."

"Yet an instill you trusted that Bitch Queen"

"I don't know what you are talking about"

"Oh well you need to sit you broke ass down! Who is in charge?"

"I'm and who are you?" Eddie responded as he stepped from behind Zac and Lil Tony.

Spotting Trapp and Crazy less easing though the back door, Neko advised them to put down their guns. Beginning to hear sirens, Neko shook his head as a sign for them to make their move. Trap shot Black in the leg and butted Rob with the back of his pistol. Crazy legs kept his two 9mm aimed at Eddie. Neko and some more of his locs came deeper into the kitchen. Eddie dropped his unload gun on the ground and dropped the duffle bag.

Making them kicking the guns away from them before they came any closer. Trap heard music coming from the exit door, "Come on that Lil K" he stated as he walked backward to the exit door. Not taking his eyes off them one bit, as he open the exit door. Lil K run inside and looked around and smiled while he grabbed two duffle bag. Crazy legs and Trap began helping him as Neko walked and forced everyone into the walking refrigerator. Shutting the door a placing a wooden spoon inside the lock hole.

Rushing over to help them as the rest of the crew went to get the cars. The louder the sirens got, the more Neko panicked. Not trying to get caught with all of that dope and money. He jumped behind the wheel of his Royal blue box Chevy and drove off. Seeing Neko hauling ass down narrow made everybody follow suit. Meanwhile Ty and Lil Tony Rammed their shoulder against the freezer door trying to break the wooden spoon.

"Aw…remember you."

"No you don't, I ain't' ever seen you before."

"Aw yes that's right, you used to date Queen"

"And who are you?"

"I'm old man Ying, you don't remember me."

"Man I don't have time for all of that bullshit"

As soon as Eddie made his statement the door came flying open. They flew out of the Refrigerator and made a run for it. As everybody separated Eddie went for the one duffle bag that was left behind. Picking the bag up and running to the back door. Running across the highway with a duffle bag striped across his shoulder. As he make it inside of the same subdivide that he did his surveillance in, he saw Rob, Lil Tony and Black get caught.

As he stood there watching the police raid the plaza a grey Honda drove up to the entrance. Eddie walked over and asked the young lady for a ride. Taking a long pause before telling him to get in.

Chapter 12

T.H.N: Sticky

While discussing prices, Sticky made sure she took a real good look at him. Knowing that she could get a better deal from her cousin Darius out in Texas. She just wanted to spread her business elsewhere.

"Aye check this out Cranberry"

"Yea I'm listening" have to meet up somewhere in the middle from now on to do business."

"Ok that's cool with me, you tell me where and I'll be there."

"Well for now let me just get four things of lean and if you ever want some real gas you let me know" Sticky spoke as she reached inside of Fend; handbag and pulled out a roll of money.

As soon as the deal was made Ked looked at him and said "I told you she was about her business." Then jumped in the car behind her. As they drove away from the meeting point, Ked turned and looked at Sticky.

"So what do you think?"

"Yea he sweet but he's just a runner"

"So you don't think it would be good to get him"

"Oh yea we most defiantly going to get him and whoever he is working for"

"Okay now we are talking"

As they hit the highway Sticky told how she would make her move and what she would give him off of it.

T.H.N: Honey

As the night time breeze blew about, Honey knew it was time to step back inside the hospital. As she entered back into Queen's room she overheard Boobie talking freaky to Queen. Cleaning her throat to let get his attention, Boobie jumped from being startled. "Oh I thought you was still outside."

"I bet you did"

"Man go head on with that."

"What I'm just saying I ain't the one talking about eating no ass."

"So you saying you ain't never had that ass licked"

"No I ain't saying all of that, I'm just saying he can't defend herself right now."

"Let me find out you hating on yo momma"

"Boy whatever that's where I get my looks from"

As they joked around a nurse walked into the room. She begin checking the EKG machine, then turned to Boobie and Honey and informed them that the visitation hours were over for the night and only one could stay. Honey looked at Boobie and said "Well we will see you later Freaky man"

"You got jokes uh"

"Just a little" Honey giggled while watching him grab his things.

Chapter 13

T.H.N: Sticky

"My nigga we been dealing with each other for almost a month now. And every time I come down I go up on my bottles, but now you can't serve me what I want or should I say need."

"Now it ain't like that, I only get so much from my plug."

"So where he at I'm trying to spend some money."

"Hold on let me call him"

"And what's up with you and these cars, every time I see you in a different rental car."

"Oh I just like to drive different stuff"

"Oh because I was praying that you wasn't an under cover."

In the middle of him about to get smart his plug picked up the phone. Motioning for Sticky to give him one minute as he walk away to talk. Sticky slowly pulls her phone out of her leg while she texted, making sure he wasn't paying her no attention.

The text: Get ready to move.

As she slipped the phone back into her pocket as she sat on the hood of the car. Cranberry walked back to the car smiling then stated today is your lucky day.

"So that mean we gone makes some money or what"

"Yea he agreed to meet with you."

"Okay cool"

"Hop in your car and follow me"

Leaving out of the Flash Food off of highway 24

headed back down to Dud land. Sticky made her call as she got on the Ramp to the expressway. Making sure everybody was on point and stayed a few cars behind them. Knowing that it would have been easy to throw him off with the cars already on the expressway. She still had to keep them on point.

T.H.N: Honey

Sitting around at the hospital playing on her phone. Honey stumbled across a party that she had forgotten all about. Seeing how everybody was getting all dressed up on Facebook and Instagram, made her realize what the day really was. Feeling stupid for forgetting that T.O Green was hosting a party at Clayton State. Everybody has been talking about it for the last two weeks. Looking over at Queen as she laid there, Honey got up sucking her teeth then stated "Girl you know I can't miss this party."

Gathering all of her things, before leaning over to kiss Queen on her forehead. As she was walking out the room, she yelled "I'll see you tomorrow ma, Love ya" then closed the door. Walking into the lobby approaching the night shift security guard.

"Excuse me can you keep an extra eye out on room 323"

"Yes Ma'am"

"Thank you kindly sirs."

Winking her eye at the guards as she walked away making her ass bounce harder than usual. As the doors opened for her to pass through, she slightly looked back to see if they were watching. Catching them behind the desk gossiping about her. Probably talking about how fat my ass is, or how they would love to fuck me. Honey thought to herself as she kept walking.

T.H.N: Sticky

Driving into a small but nice Trailer park. Sticky scanned the area as she drove through. Looking for any other exit route beside the one she came in on. Also looking for any trailer that might be a stash spot Passing a tan trailer on the right hand side with burglar bars on it. Sticky knew that had to be a spot for something.

Having the phone on her lap as she pointed out things to John-John. Parking at the next trailer over confirmed what Sticky was thinking. When she had turned her car around, she saw guys coming out of trailer going into the other. Relaying everything to John-John before sliding the phone into her front pocket. Grapping the small Prada duffle hand bag off the passenger seat. Before she got out the car she made sure she had a bullet in the chamber and John-John knew what the go code was.

Making sure he kept his phone on mute, so he could hear her loud and clean. Sticky put her phone back in her pocket and place the nine millimeter in the center of her lower back. Sticky got out of the car and tossed the bag on her shoulder.

"Nice little set up you got here."

"Oh yea this the big home's."

"Oh tats what's up, go do he rent them out."

"Yeah he is all about his paper just like you"

Walking inside the trailer Cranberry greeted the two guys that was sitting in the living room before asking for Prime time.

"He's back in the back with some trick" Redeye told him as he got off the sofa and walking into the kitchen.

"Yo prime! It's me Cranberry old girl out here waiting"

Coming out the bedroom in nothing but a robe made Cranberry laugh and Sticky turned her head. Come on dawn put some clothes on you look like a shaved bird with you skinny self. Cranberry joined as Prime time came down the hallway.

"Prime time this is....Damn girl what your name is again?"

"Child we been doing business for how long now and you forgot my nigga. It Star"

"Oh yea I knew it was something with a S."

Looking at Primetime as he stood there checking Sticky out. Sticky knew that he was high as hell. His eyes was super grassy and his nose had a slight run to it.

"So are we going to stand around all day or do business?"

"I like you already, so let's get to it."

Conducting small talking as they went over numbers, Sticky was able to slide the code word into their conversation. Prime time told his guys to grab six causes of the lean and one bag of the ICE. They left out of his trailer and over to the tan one. Standing there waiting for them to get back, a loud "Daddy what are you doing? I can't keep playing in this pussy without you" came from the bedroom. Primetime looked at Sticky and Cranberry smiling then told them that he would be right back.

"Man come on bruh that bitch can wait."

"Shiid we still got to wait for them to come back over with the product."

"Doug there you go with that high shit."

"Well nigga go check on them then" Prime time yelled aggressively Cranberry Shook his head as he walked out the door.

T.H.N: Cranberry

"Man I'm so sick out this nigga with that high shit." Cranberry spoke out loud to himself as he walked down the stairs. Not paying attention to the nigga that was coming from under the steps. All he felt was hard hitting him across the head before he hit the ground. Rolling over to his side trying to see who or what hit him. He caught a kick to the face knocking him out cold. John-John quickly restrained Cranberry and dragged him under the steps.

T.H.N: Sticky

Peeping through the small crack in door before busting it wide open. Sending shots through a small threw pillow, that she had done picked up off the sofa. Hitting him in his chest two time before aiming the gun and pillow at thick black chick.

"Bitch where the money at?"

"It all I the other trailer, please don't kill me"

"So it ain't nothing in this house."

"Yeah it's a small safe in the closet under some clothes"

"Thank you" Sticky cried out before putting one in her head.

Running inside the closet spotting the pale of clothes off the dribble. Sticky removed the clothes found two safe, one small tan one that was sitting on top of a medium size black one. Picking them both up and quickly toted them to the living room. As soon as she sat them down the front door opened. Her eye opened wide and her mouth dropped. She forgot to grab the pistol from off the dresser.

When she realized that it was only John-John, she took a deep breath. John-John gave her a look of disappointment knowing that she was just down bad from the look on her face.

"Where they at?"

"They in the back."

"Ok cool go grab a small trash bag and grab all you can."

Sticky took off running through the house.

T.H.N: John-John

Making his way to the bedroom, seeing both victims with bullet hole in them. He pulled the black Nike book bag off his back and took out a glass bottle. Picking up the guy's hands and poured the liquid substance on them. As the acid ate away his fingers, John-John poured some more on to his body and did the chick the same way. Smiling as he watched the acid eat away their body. Always being amazed how the acid just eats away everything that it touches.

Wiping off the bottle before putting it back into his book bag. He spotted the shell causing on the floor, he picked them up and called sticky back into the room.

"Baby this you second time."

"What I do?"

Opening his hand to show her the shell causing. Feeling bad for getting caught slipping twice today, she knew he wasn't going to let it go. He just looked at her then told her to get everything out of the house. She took off running back to the front of the house. John-John stepped back into the hallway and grab the gas container off the floor. And started slinging gas throughout the house.

Going out the front door behind Sticky, Leaving a trail of gasoline behind them both. Making sure Sticky got a head start away from the scene before he lit the trail of gasoline. Hoping into a black on black Nissan Titan XD. "Ride nigga Ride" John-John yelled form the back seat as he looked out the back window. Watching both trailer go up in flames.

"Bruh them country niggas was strapped."

"Yea, so how much you think we got."

"Man I can't even say, How much you think it was Fly?"

"Shild all I know is we gone be straight with whatever it is"

Feeling good form a job well done, John-John grabbed Gregg and Fly around the neck and gave them a sarcastic.

"I love you guys". Fly Turned around in the seat as John-John sat back, and gave him a silly look before bursting out saying "Man if you don't sit you corny ass down." They all busted out laughing as they hit the highway.

T.H.N: Honey

Not hearing form Sticky all day made Honey wonder where she was at, and if she knew about the party. But as she parked the car, she realized that they were all part of the same click. Smiling at herself for having a slow moment, while making sure her makeup was intact. Grabbing her purse before hopping out the car. Before walking inside of the gym, she send out a text to Sticky. Telling her that she was at the party at Clayton State and she needed get to come.

Put the phone back inside of her purse as walked inside of the gym. The place was packed and it was only 9:30 pm. Walking around the gym checking everyone out, trying to see who was even closet to her dress code. Having on a cream color Prada one piece, with a gold chain belt hanging around her waste. Some off while high heel times with some gold hoop ear rings, and a three layer diamond necklace that she made the niggas and batches turn their heads. Her ass was bouncing so hard in that body suit you couldn't help but to look. As the party turned up, she got loose. Having a crowd form a circle around her as she put on a show. Making her ass clap while in a full split, then getting up and making both cheeks move one at a time. Bending all the way over touching her toes, then dropping low and coming back up.

Dancing the night away, T.O Green came over the Mic "Cut the music! I got something special for all tonight. I got one of my squid niggas here to amp this thanks up one more notch." Waka Flocka came out one to the stage and did his verse to No Hands, then crank it up with Kebo Gotti and Cap with Grove St party and O Let's do it. As the crowd got hipped, Honey eased her way to the Restroom. The liquor was running through her.

T.H.N: Sticky

Stepping inside of the gym bobbing her head to the music, while scanning the area for Honey. John-John squeezed her on the butt then whispered in her ear before walking off. She knows that he wasn't going to stay around long. Taking out her phone to call Honey as she moved around on the dance floor. Everyone that knew her kept pushing up on her telling how lite Honey was. But no one could tell her where she was at.

Constantly calling her phone but not receiving answer, made Sticky feel as if she was up to her hoeish ways. Beginning to loosen up as the music played, she couldn't stop smiling at John-John up on stage acting a fool. Feeling the vibration of her cell going off. She pulled the phone out of her pocket and seen one missed call. Opening the call to see who it was, the screen read Honey. Hitting the call button to see where she was.

Hearing screaming coming from the other end of the phone made her panic. It wasn't a sexual scream that was coming through the phone. Pushing her way through the crowd trying her best to get to the exit door. Stepping out outside yelling hello into the phone, Sticky heard a loud commotion coming from behind the Gym.

Hearing someone yelling out stop into the phone made her more suspicious.

Beginning to walk toward the back of the Gym, she saw and unmarked black van speeding off. Not hearing a word on the other end of the phone, she knew shit just went south. As she stood at the back of the Gym, two females that was attending the part approached her.

"Sticky they got your sister" They both cried out. Placing her hand on her head trying not to cry. Sticky looked over at the two chicks and asked them if they saw who it was.

"They looked like they was Asian"

"Ok call the police and tell them everything I'm going after them" Sticky said as she took off for her car.

T.H.N: Queen

The sound of the EKG machine going off, made the nurses Rush to the room. Seeing her heart Rate going up and her body covered in sweat. They begin to follow medical procedures. And within seconds Queen popped up in the bed yelling out for hope. Trying to get her to come down and stop moving. But all she kept doing was yelling out for her daughters, while trying to get out of bed.

Not understanding how she was able to move like that, when she was fresh out a coma. The nurses called for help to restrain her to the bed. Not wanting to hurt her or for her to hurt herself. Finally getting her to come down, one of the nurses asked her what was going on and who was Hope and Santana.

"My daughters I need to see them"

"Ok Ma'am I will try to call them for you."

As the nurse left out the room Detective Patterson came waling into the room. Pulling out a small note pad as he walked towards the bed. Hello Ms. Arm wood, I'm detective Patterson and I would like to ask you a few question, if you feel u to it.

"I'm sorry but I don't talk to the police."

"Well Ma'am I'm just here to help."

"Help with what?"

"We are trying to see if Eddie Ward is behind all of this."

"All of what?"

"Your place getting broke into and you getting hit by acre and left for dead."

"I don't know what to tell you sir."

"Well Ms. Adam tells us that you and Eddie used to date and he couldn't stop talking about how he was going to pay you back."

Queen sat there looking crazy as the detective kept going on and on about Eddie. She knew it would be slim to non-chances of them finding him. He had just as many connects as she did. And you really had to think outside the box if you wanted him. As the detective kept going on and on with slick ways to get her to talk. Queen still didn't say a word, she begin think to herself why would he want all this time to get back at her. He was just as dangerous as she was.

Hushing the detective up so she could pay attention to the news.

T.H.N: News Reporter.

We are reporting live here at Clayton State College. Where it seems to be a kidnapping that just took place. They are saying that the victim name is Hope Arm wood also known as Honey. She's 27 years old and she was a student here at the College. Everyone that attended this party here tonight said that she was the life of the party. And no one seen her for a while once she went to the rest room. Hold that thought Carl we have two eye witnesses here that wants to go unarmed.

"What did you see happen here tonight."

"Well we was out back taking us smoke break, when we see like six or seven again struggling to tote something that was wrapped it a black sheet."

"So you are not sure that it was hope."

"Yeah I'm sure because we heard her scream out help and she was moving around trying to break free."

"Oh yeah girl don't forget to tell them about the black Van they drove away."

Well there you have it Carl, I'm Vanessa Love reporting live from Clayton State College. Thank you Vanessa for that great update. Earlier today we had a shooting or an Arm Robbery gone bad that took place in Lawrenceville. Could the owner of that shop be the same ones behind the kidnapping?

"That's a good question Carl, but I'm pretty sure the police are all over it."

T.H.N: Queen

"Damn!"

"What was that Ms. Armwood?"

"Nothing I'm just worried about my child"

"Well you need to tell me everything that you know so I can help"

"Sir I don't know nothing I've been in here for however long I been here."

"Ok I'm just say it would go a lot faster with your help."

"Look I just need to get out of here and go home."

"If you agree to helping us I will see about getting you released tomorrow."

Sitting up in the bed, Queen looked at the detective then asked if she was under arrest or anything. He paused for a minute then responded with a polite no Ma'am your free to go. Picking up the hospital I phone and proceeded to call Sticky.

"Hello"

"Sticky come get me"

"Who is this?"

"Girl its your damn Momma."

"Oh my God Ma is it really you?"

"Yes girl and where are you at?"

"I trailing behind the people that got Honey"

"Oh my God Sticky be careful where you are?"

"Umm it seems to be like some ware house of sugar leaf parkway."

Hanging up the phone Sticky and begin Climbing out of bed. Looking around he room for some old clothes to put on. She opened a small closet space that they normally have extra hospital dresses at. And found one of her duffle bags. Picking it up and going through it, she found a pair of sweats and T-shirt and Tennis Shoes. Quality sliding on the sweats pants and shoe, before telling the officer to turn his head. Once she was dressed she told the detective if he wanted to help he would give her a ride.

Chapter 14

T.H.N: Honey

Sitting hope Lesley tied to chair yelling for help. A small Asian man dressed in suit and tie approached her. Walking around her in a circle, as he Rubbed his hand through her hair and down her face. Trying her best to move her head to keep him from playing in it. He got mad and gripped her by the hair and pulled her head back. Then straddled her and licked the side of her face.

"You like that you dirty little whore."

"Get off me you little dick bastard and let me go."

"Now is that how you talk to someone that has your life in their hands"

"What do you want from me you prick?"

"You know what I want from you"

"Well if its pussy that you want, you need to get on back page"

"No No No my child I want my money and drugs back."

"What! I don't know what you are talking about"

"You don't want to talk, let's see if this changes your mind."

Un straddling himself from her legs then Round house Kicking her across the face. Instantly drawing blood from the force of the kick. As the blood dripped down her face from the cut over her right cheek bone. Honey closed her eyes and thought about what would Sticky do. And before she knew she was talking more shit then a little bit. Hopping around in the chair telling him to let her go, so she could whoop his ass.

He begun laughing at her as he rolled up his sleeves. Six more again dressed in Trap suits walked in the room.

"Oh you are the little bitches that kidnapped me."

"Your pretty tuff for a chick, just like your Momma"

"Don't talk about my momma."

"Oh no me and Queen go way back."

"Well if you know my momma why in the hell you got me here."

"Because she had someone hit my spot"

Going back and fort with him about how Queen wasn't able to set him up. Feeling that it was all lies he send his crew to grab the supplies.

T.H.N: Sticky

Changing into the black T and grey sweat pants, that she kept in the trunk of her car. Before shutting the trunk she lifted up the carpet and pulled out a bullet proof vest and a drake with two extended clips. Making her way closer to the wear house. Trying her best to spot any cameras on the rundown buildings. Peeking inside of the a jarred door before easing her way on the inside. Using the lighten form the outside light poles that shined inside the building, to find her way around the building.

Hearing the Asian speak their native language, she knew she was closer to honey. Panicking inside her mind with thoughts of her life about to end. She took a deep breath as her adrenaline ran wild. Coming around the corner feeling like she was moving in slow motion as she up the strip. Squeezing the trigger as the bullets wrung out. All of the Asian distrusted into different direction. Catching some of them before they could hide behind old wear house objects.

As the others returned fire, Sticky ducked and dodged behind objects as well until she was able to take them down getting hit two times in the chest knocked the wind out of her. Leaning up against some old barrels trying to catch her breathe. She peeked around the barrels and laid down some cover fire, as she took off to the small office room. As she made it inside of the office she realized that she just cornered herself in. But the only good thing she noticed was that she could see the whole area that she was in.

As bullets came flying through the small room, Sticky hided behind a table that was flipped over. Firing back out of the room before flipping her clip around. Having them duck taped together made it a lot easier for her. Everything got quiet, all she could hear were footsteps running away from her. Lifting up to look out of the small window. She saw them head for the exit door.

Releasing fires as she walked closer to the window. Hitting one in the back of the head. Another one in the left side of his back. While only grazing the other one on the neck.

T.H.N: Queen

"Look I appreciate the lift but you have to say out of this."

"What do you mean? I'm a cop, I'm going to do my job."

"I know what you are, but the thing is I don't involve cops into my life."

"Well it's too late now, we are here and I'm all you got."

Looking at detective Patterson with a frown on her face, knowing that she just went against everything she ever stood for. Climbing out of the car and running over to Stick's Honda. Looking inside the windows trying to see if anyone was inside Hearing gun shots coming from inside the building, Officer Paterson rushed over to shield Queen. Not knowing if they were getting shot at, at that moment or if it was all on the inside.

Squatting beside the car detective Patterson stuck. Admiring Queen's beauty as they waited beside the car.

Catching him in a daze, Queen snapped her fingers and cleared her throat.

"Umm it's no time for that sir."

"Oh damn I'm sorry, your right lets go."

Slowly coming up form beside the car, detective Patterson told Queen to stay put. Running back to his unmarked car and popped the trunk. Snatching his extra vest out, then shut his trunk. Placing it over her clothes before grabbing her hand, so he could lead the way. Before they entered the building, Queen stopped Patterson and asked if he was going to call for back up.

"I thought you didn't like the cops in your business."

"I don't but I just thought..."

Stopping herself before she said something crazy. But liking the fact that he wasn't going to involve the police beside himself. He waited to see if she was going to finish her sentence before heading inside the building. As the sun rose the building became more lite careful walking through the building following the sound of the gun shots.

T.H.N: Honey

"Looks like someone here to save you."

"Thank you Jesus, because I don't know how much long I could keep that up."

"It's ok I'll finish the job myself"

Pulling out a small hunting knife from his back pocket. Flipping it open and running the blade gently down her face. As he walked around her cutting in different areas, he asked if she ever heard of dead by a thousand cuts. Screaming for help as she tried to break free. Not wanting to get cut again. Hearing him talk about how good of a business partner Queen was didn't make it any better.

It was like his trip down memory lane, made him murder for her crossing him. Beginning to make his next cut sticky walked into the room.

"Don't even think about."

"Ah! Little sister to the recuse."

Before he could finish his remark sticky released two shots. Hitting him in the shoulder and leg, Making him drop the knife. Rushing over to Honey and kicking the knife far away from them as possible. Looking at Honey dripping in blood made sticky even murder. She turned around and shot him two more time. Dropping him to his knees delivered a kick straight to the face.

As he rolled over to his back Sticky begun stomping him. Watching him spit up blood with every kick she delivered to the chest. Mumbling to herself as she started kicking faster and harder.

"Sticky! Sticky! Santana stop!" Honey cried out

Fuck dis again bastard he tried to kill you."

"Stop for me please and come untie me"

Taking one last kick before away Shaking her head as she united Honey form chair, thinking to herself. Soon as Sticky untried the last Rope, Honey jumped out of the chair and gave her a huge hug. Their emotions were all over the place. Excited from being reunited, but sad for not being able to get there fast enough. Hearing the sound of broken glass, Sticky opened her eyes and lifted her gun.

Seeing a silhouette of a tall figured person walking to the room. Sticky made it known that she would shoot if they came any closer. Hearing a familiar voice come from out the shadow as they came closer, Sticky lowered her gun. Seeing Queen some running form out the darkness put a big smile on her face. Her and Honey took of running to meet her half way. Embracing each other with love, as Queen shook her head at the cuts Honey had.

"Ma who is that?"

"Oh that's detective Peterson."

"Oh my God Ma, I know you didn't bring the police with."

"Sticky it's ok I think he likes me" Queen giggled

Making their way toward detective Patterson and the exit, He told sticky that it was cool. Tucking away the drake but still kept an eye on the detective. As they made their way back to the car, Honey stopped and looked at Queen.

"Ma who are you?"

"Girl what are you talking about?"

"I'm just saying we have been through at lot within these last few months"

"Yeah I know it's a lot trying to keep this shit together."

Sticky shouted out.

As they got into the car Queen told them to hold on. Walking to the back of the car, where detective Patterson stood there waiting.

"Well I guess this means I'll be seeing you soon."

"Yea I guess so"

"You got my number right"

"Yeah I do but it wouldn't be hard to find you."

Queen lead in and gave him a kiss on the lips and a hug good bye.

Squeezing him tightly before letting him go as she rubbed the private part of his pants. Seeing his brain fragment coming out of his head with in seconds of letting him go. Screaming as she ran back to the car. Sticky jumped out of the car releasing the rest of her clip, into the direction she thought the shot came from. Hopping back into the car and having ass trying to make a clean get away.

"Ma you alright?!"

"Yeah I'm good baby"

"Honey you good?!"

"Yeah I'm ok just a little cut up."

"Damn I was feeling him too, I thought I was gone get me some"

"Ugh ma you nasty" They both yelled out.

As they headed back to the Southside, they shared with Queen everything that's been going on.

Chapter 15

T.H.N: Sticky

"Damn it feels good to have everything back to normal." Sticky thought to herself as she sat on the edge of her bed. Looking around her trying to see what she wanted to do first. Noticing that it was after 2 o'clock, she realized that she was late for appointment. Reaching over to the other side of the bed to grab her phone. Seeing two miss calls and one text from John-John.

Sticky forgot all about their plans. Quickly send out two text one to Ked and the other to John-John. Sitting her phone down then waked to her closet, pulling out three big black duffle bags.

"Damn is all that you."

"Honey is all that you."

"Honey what I done told you about sneaking into my room."

"That ass mighty fat with you bent over like that"

"Girl my ass fat anyways but what do you want?"

"Oh momma wants us at her house in ten minutes."

"Ok you little freak you can close my door now"

"You should let me tap that ass I'll show you how it's done."

"Ugh Honey you so damn nasty."

"Girl I was just play but be ready in ten."

Standing there in her bra and panties waiting for Honey to shut her door. Son as the door shut she unzipped all of the duffle bags. Taking out two pounds of sour diesel out one bag, two things of lean out of the other and five thousand dollars ut the last bag. Placing them all inside of Queen's little duffle bag before going to freshen.

T.H.N: Queen

Preparing lunch while talking on the phone and waiting for the girls to come over. Tears rolled down her face. Thinking about all they have been through. Queen hung up the phone and took a minute to get herself together. Wiping tears from her eyes as she heard the door open.

"Ma where you at?"

"I'm still in the kitchen baby"

"Oh okay is lunch ready yet."

"Just about but where is Santana"

"She was getting dressed"

Knowing that Sticky haven't changed one bit brought a smile on her face. Earing a car pull up in front of the house, made Queen look out the kitchen widow. Not being able to see inside of the car because of the dark tint. She grabbed old trustee out of the kitchen cabinet and placed the 357 on the counter. Waiting to see what they were up to, she seen Sticky coming out of the house and the window start to let down. Taking off for the front door.

T.H.N: Sticky

Making her way down the driveway, she noticed that someone in the passenger seat kept moving. Shaking her head and smiling at her little cousin. Before she could say a word Queen and Honey had done busted out the house yelling Sticky turned her head and looked at them with puzzled look. They stopped and stood there for a second looking at each other before Sticky asked them what was wrong.

Queen wrapped her arm around Honey and turned to go back inside. Raising her hand with the 357 in it, shaking it as a sign that she still mean business. Sticky put her hand over her face and shook her head. Looking back into the car to finish business, it was like ked didn't miss a beat. He still was getting served up like ain't nothing happen.

"Boy you are wild and who car is this"

"It's mine, it's the new scot cat and its paid for."

"I'm feeling this color to, but here is something off that little. Jug we pulled in Dud land."

"Ooow shit girl suck this dick, oh I'm sorry cuz but I'm good on money me and my crew got a new hustle going on. Easy money!"

Sticky reached inside the bag and pulled out the roll of money. Placed it in her pocket then threw the duffle bag on the back seat. Watching her little cousin force the chick's head down while he moaned out he was cumming. She knew that he wasn't the same little cousin that she used to babysit. He had done became a man. As the chick got up and stuck her head out the window, Ked introduced her.

"Sticky this Paris, Paris this my cousin Sticky."

"I done seen you before."

"Yeah I work at Southern Regional Hospital."

"Umm that's right you just look all different with all of that going on."

Bending back down to look inside the car, Sticky told Ked to hit her up later so he could bring her up to speed with the new hustle. Watching how the sun hit the maroon paint as he drove away. She knew she had to step her game up. Entering inside of the house to see Queen and Honey standing there waiting on her.

T.H.N: Queen

"Which one of your little boyfriends was that?"

"That was Ked our cousin."

"Oh well why didn't he come in?"

"He has too much going on right now."

"Hell I almost shot his little bad ass."

Smelling the aroma of some fried chicken baked in Texas Pete hot sauce. Sticky went straight for the kitchen, by passing Queen and Honey. Sticking her hand inside the blow of homemade French fries. Queen chased her out of the kitchen so she could fix their plates. Once they all sat down Queen looked at them before she began to speak.

"You know I love yall right?"

"Duh? Ma of course we know you love us" Honey replied

"But where are you going with this" Sticky added

"Well that's what I'm about to tell y'all, so listen up. Y'all know that I have been doing this since the 80's. I have done it all from pimping, Robbing and hustling. And it's time for me to sit down and enjoy life. Now we have plenty of money in some off shores accounts and we also have stock investment. But what I'm really getting at here is....It's up to you girls if you want to take over what I started, or do your own thing. Sticky I really would love for you to take over because you are just like me in so many ways. I will give you all of my connections and everything. And they all will respect you just like they do me. So the choice is your."

"Why you want her to run it? I can handle business to"

"Baby if you want' it you can have it, but just don't be looking for help."

"I don't want to do it I was just asking."

"That's why right there, you not built for that life style."

Sitting there not saying a word as she pulled the chicken breast a part. Thinking to herself what just happen. She was given the opportunity that she always wanted. But now feeling that it was too much for her to handle. As she continued to block out Queen and Honey fussing about her street cried. She finished her meal and got up from the table. Hearing Queen all her name as walked out the door.

Standing on the porch to get some fresh air to clear her mind, before she made her decision. Knowing that to paste the porch a cherry red BMW drove into the driveway. Stopping in the middle of her tracks to see who was inside the car. As the driver door open, she saw some all-white Gucci loafers hit the ground. Waiting to see who or what was next, Boobie came climbing out of the car.

Holding his head shaking his dreads before throwing his head back. Gripping his dreads and placed them inside of ta rubber band. Stepping on to the porch Boobie smiled at Sticky as he took off his Gucci shades.

"Ok nigga I see you in your all white Gucci fit, but who you here for."

"Really?! Come on man you know I'm here for yo Momma."

"Well yeah I know that but I didn't know you guys was talking"

"Oh yeah Honey hooked it up this morning so we could go out."

"Who that bitch think she is Dr. Phil or somebody."

Boobie started laughing and the front door came flying open. They both looked at the door, Honey was standing there with her hand on her hip.

"Here she come now Bobie" Honey stated as she step to the side.

"Watching Queen walk to the door was like Heaven. Everything got bright around her and doves started flying. Standing there with his mouth open

He had done blocked out everything around him.

He knew they was going to stop traffic together. With him being young fly nigga and just being a bad bitch. Snapping out of it as she grabbed him by the hand.

"Damn you are gorgeous."

"Why thank you, are you ready to go?"

"Aye I'm ready."

Leading Queen to the car, Boobie looked back at Sticky and Honey over his shades then smiled.

T.H.N: Sticky

"Have you thought about what you was going to do?"

"You heard momma, it's time for me to pick up where she left off."

"Well if you ever need me I'm here for you sis!"

"I know hope you are always there when I need in some kind of way. But I'm going to do thing a little bit different this time around." Sticky said while Rubbing her hands together. Looking around at her neighborhood as a million thoughts run through her head. Following Honey back inside the house, then turn around to take one last look.

"The world is mine" She mumbled to herself before shutting the door.

The End

Printed in the United States
by Baker & Taylor Publisher Services

Printed in the United States
by Baker & Taylor Publisher Services